Shelter In The Sun

Shelter In The Sun

By
Shelbi Walker

Shelter In The Sun
A Love Story

ISBN: 978-0-578-33688-6

FIRST EDITION

First Printing 2021

Printed in the United States of America
Library of Congress Cataloging in Publication Data on file.

Published by
Circle Square Services
Corona, California
circlesquareservices.com

CIRCLE SQUARE

Dedicated to all who have loved and lost.
You are allowed to love again.

1

Wires and Lines

It was over. Our four-year battle with Lung Cancer was over. I watched as the nurses disconnected him from the tubes and wires that were designed to give him his life back. The staff skillfully untwisted, flipped, and pulled them away from his motionless, rigoring body. So many tubes and wires. He looked like the back of the television console in our family room. I had dusted back there once and got tangled in the spaghetti mess of cords and plugs. A few wires were disconnected, and I had no idea where they came from. I plugged them into any available hole, one-by-one, but the TV would not turn on until our son-in-law, James, came over and fixed my feeble attempt at correction. Each of those wires held a specific function and their collective combination allowed us to watch some of our favorite movies and TV shows. I remember how we cried as we experienced Barack Obama making his first State of the Union address, and laughed at the home movies of our family that were, as Nia said, "casting from her phone." I didn't know what that meant then, or now, but I loved seeing her little toddling legs move cautiously through our front yard right on our TV screen. No one could fix the tangled mess this time. Like the back of the television console, I watched my husband's disconnection. I studied where every wire had come from out of his body.

The nurses moved like ballerinas, gracefully pulling and releasing him from the machines, in silence and with reverence. No one rushed me out of the room. I stayed and observed quietly taking in the dance. The last that remained was his breathing tube. Mouth agape, they drew the long tube out of him. He lay still and hollow. The life saving measures had failed. The nurses and doctors worked with precision and detail to disconnect him from the oxygen and the IVs. Their dance lasted for about 30 minutes, and then, in a flash, they were all gone. The slow death march that the hospital personnel did as they exited his room reminded me of the pictures of his days in the service. Those old photographs he would share showed him neatly pressed in his military uniform, standing erect and in line with his fellow soldiers. The emergency room doctor who attended to him was the last to leave. He was a young African American man with the build of a football player. I could see the regret in his eyes as he passed by me and offered a sincere, "I'm so sorry. We did everything we could." I thanked him. He shook my hand and patted me gently on the shoulder before retreating to the hallway to try to save another life.

The slow procession of nurses down the hallway was the only signal needed to indicate what just happened in our family. I could hear the faint cries of Corrine, while I was in a stark white room watching Sam, breathless and lifeless. In that moment, I was alone. Not in the way that causes one to believe they need to have people around them, but rather, alone in my heart. Alone in my thoughts. I could have had a crowd of people around me, chanting my name, but I would still feel alone.

Fifty years, 4 months and 27 days. That is how long Sam and I have been married. The click of the machines going off reverberated through my body like an earthquake. With every click, I felt like I was disconnecting from him and our life together. Was I dreaming? That was it. I was dreaming. This was not real. I would awaken and open my eyes and see him breathing deeply, in our bed, then turn to me and say, "Good morning gorgeous," as he had always done before Cancer took his lungs away 4 years ago. I leaned against the wall near the hospital room door and closed my eyes as tightly as I could. I saw pink sparkles behind my lids and felt the tinge of a headache. My prayer was that when I opened my eyes, Sam's death would have just been a terrible nightmare. I counted to 20 as I stood still and rigid, frozen like Lot's wife when she turned into a pillar of salt having dared to look back after escaping Sodom and Gomorrah, keeping my now aching eyelids closed. I slowly reopened them, and as the blur of my sight turned clear, I realized that I was still in the hospital room, and Sam was still lying on a gurney, dead.

My whole life as a wife and mother and grandmother was turning off. How was I to live without him? How could anyone expect me to live without him? Lost in my thoughts, I barely noticed my daughter walking into the room. Her face was tarnished with tears. The salt had stained her brown skin and it made it look like they were dry, white caverns resting on her cheeks. I could tell that she wanted to say something to me but didn't have the words.

"Mom? Are you OK?" Corrine asked.

"I don't know honey. I don't know if I'm OK, I don't know if I'll ever be OK."

I touched Sam's foot that was growing cold. I ran my hand up his leg, to his hip, and finally to his shoulders and looked at his face as he lay motionless, without breath or life. I leaned down and whispered in his ear, "I love you Sam, I've always loved you. Rest well, my sweet husband." I kissed Sam gently on the forehead and turned away.

I watched as my daughter passed me to say her final goodbyes to her father. I didn't turn back to see what she did, and I didn't attune my ear to what she said. Instead, I grabbed the Chanel handbag and clutched the soft, black, quilted leather to my chest. The gold double "Cs" felt cold against my décolletage, as it pressed hard just above the zipper of my hooded sweatshirt. Sam had bought the purse for me as a Christmas gift, the year before he got sick. I had never been a person that indulged in designer clothes or expensive handbags. It's not something that I would have purchased for myself, but I appreciated the gift and carried it everyday.

I reached for my coat that was haphazardly draped on a chair, and my keys dropped from the pocket to the floor. I bent down to pick them up and I touched the tip of Sam's Nike tennis shoes that were tucked, neatly under the bed. I had brought them with me because I intended for him to walk out of the hospital. He had episodes like this before, and he always recovered, and was able to walk out of the hospital on his own. Our dashes to the emergency room were routine and familiar. That's what happens when you have Lung Cancer. You are consumed by every breath, not knowing which one will be your last. Because our hospital visits were so frequent, I decided to keep an ER bag in each of our cars, just in case we had to rush to Hilbrand Hospital.

Sam has always been concerned about his appearance and even

during his stays in the hospital, he had to be stylish. This time was no different. In his labored breath, the day before he fell incurably ill, he insisted that I put his Pegasus Nike's in my car to replace the other shoes that were in the ER bag. Once, before we created the ER bag, I brought him an old pair of gardening clogs to wear when he was released from the hospital. He clomped out of Hilbrand less than pleased. I learned my lesson – always keep a pair of Nike's in the car for Sam.

The last thing I remember was seeing his shoes as I reached for my fallen keys. I don't recall much of what happened after that moment. In what felt like an instant, I was waking up in my bed, our bed. The room was dark and extraordinarily warm. I could see my daughter's silhouette in the distance sitting on the chair that Sam and I had bought at an antique store in Solvang in 1994. It was a trip for couples to explore the charming Dutch town located just outside of Santa Barbara, California. We ate chocolate chip pancakes in the morning, and drank cappuccinos at night. During the day, we traversed the small quaint streets and fell in love again. After a robust breakfast one morning, we spotted the chair in the window of a tiny, cramped shop that sold everything from jewelry to handmade greeting cards. The chair reminded us of a painting that hung in our home when we first married. It was a forest-scape that was painted in oil on canvas. The chair was solid oak and the seat was covered in a woven tapestry that depicted a winter forest scene. We loved it and had it shipped to our home where it has been for decades.

"Mom? You have been asleep for a couple of hours. How are you feeling?" Corrine's voice was shaky and pensive.

I rubbed my eyes and thought to myself, *Sleep? For a couple of hours?* I could not imagine that I had been sleep for as long as I had. It was dark outside, and the house was quiet. I suppose the stress of the day had taken over and I passed out right there on the hospital floor beneath where my husband lay. Corrine said that I woke up and the doctors checked me out and then gave me medicine to help me sleep. She had taken me home to help me sleep off the horror of the day.

"The doctor said to call as soon as you woke up. I am going to call him to let him know that you're OK. Are you hungry?" Corrine asked.

I struggled to grasp the words that she was saying. My mind was foggy and I could feel my pulse behind my eyes.

"No sweetie I'm not hungry, I'm hurting." That was all the conversation that I could muster.

Corrine walked softly toward my bedside. Laying in our bed, I could still smell Sam's scent to my left. He had always slept to my left. His Bipap machine was on the nightstand and I could see the dent in his pillow where his head was, just 24 hours before. I knew in that moment that I could no longer sleep there. It had been our bed for years and now I was in it all by myself, alone. I sat up mumbling to myself, "First thing tomorrow morning, I have to get rid of this bed." I needed Nia and a few of her friends to move it out of the house.

"Where is Nia?" I asked. Corrine answered with a different tone. Nia had always caused her to speak with a different tone.

"Mom, you know Nia -- here today gone tomorrow. I'll try to reach her on her cell phone."

I knew why my granddaughter was not there. It wasn't because she didn't care for me or want to be there for me in this time, but rather, because of, Corinne, her mother. She was not the most loving toward Nia, and their relationship was challenging for both of them. Nia was a free spirit who loved to just live. I had raised Corinne in a way that was more traditional. Her life was regimented and structured. Sam had demanded that everything in our home be in order, including our daughter. Corrine was rarely out of line and she carried that extreme measure of control into her own wifehood and motherhood. Corinne never knew how to have fun, and Nia was her direct opposite. Nia was a party, all the time. She lived her life unrestrained and free. I loved watching her operate in the world.

"I swear that girl is going to give me fits. She's 26 years-old and is still chasing this dream of having some gym." Corrine lamented.

I turned my head away from Corrine. I didn't want to hear about my granddaughter or her frustration with her that day. I just wanted to sit with the fact that my husband was gone and never coming back.

Lung Cancer is a nasty disease. It robs you of your breath and quality of life almost instantly. Sam used to describe it like a constant sense of drowning. He could never catch his breath. Sam was stubborn and he paid the ultimate price. When he entered boot camp, he picked up smoking. He knew it was bad for his body, but in those days, in the military, every soldier smoked. He quit after Corrine was born. He had to. Corrine was born premature and was a severe asthmatic. In those days, doctors didn't have any real treatments for asthma, but they were astute enough to realize that tobacco smoke and respiratory disease was a bad combination. We believed that Sam's smoking, all those years ago, was the cause of his Cancer. We were wrong.

My husband had worked 40 years in the aerospace industry as a mechanical engineer. He earned a Bachelor of Science degree in Mathematics from Lincoln University in Pennsylvania, then attended the University of Michigan where he earned a Master of Science degree in Mechanical Engineering. He was a brilliant man who provided for his family. When he was hired to work at Houghton Aerospace right out of graduate school, and he became the lead engineer in the space and defense department. While he was building his career, he asked me to forfeit mine in teaching to stay home to take care of him. That did not happen. I had my own life plan and it didn't include cooking, cleaning, and doting over my husband and fulfilling his needs. I hated that he worked at Houghton. It was a large conglomerate that didn't offer him reasonable time off. He worked all the time. His time in the labs at Houghton were filled with metal plating and testing insulation. He spent days in those enclosed areas where he likely inhaled the particulate matter that ultimately destroyed his lungs. He was diagnosed with Lung Cancer 4 years ago. Six rounds of chemotherapy and radiation were not enough to stave off the vicious, unrelenting plague of Cancer. I hoped that the management at Houghton would send a card or floral arrangement, but I doubted that they would.

Something as simple as a common cold would require an emergency room visit and could be lethal to Sam. That fateful day, we went to the hospital because he had a lingering sniffle and nagging cough. It turned out to be a sinus infection and he was prescribed antibiotics. The sniffle went away, but the cough never ended. We attributed the delay in healing to the postnasal drip and the raspy cough to the sinusitis, but later we discovered that his lungs had just started to give out. The night before his death, he lay on our bed struggling to breathe. He was hooked up to his oxygen tank and the wispy sound of air going in and out of his lungs lulled me to sleep. At about 4:00 in the morning, I was awakened to the sound of the rattle and rails of his lungs. I turned to see if he was still breathing, but he was struggling harder than ever. His eyes were fixed to the sky. I jumped out of bed with my cell phone in hand to call 9-1-1. The ambulance arrived and rushed him to the hospital, where they attempted to revive him for an hour. They were unsuccessful. My husband died just as the sun was coming up at 5:48 AM. And now, I lay in our bed, the same bed, with the same sheets, with the scent of my Sam lingering in the air.

Corinne had always been a caretaker, and this season of our life was no different. She stayed at our house for a week after her father died. She graciously went with me to the funeral home where we made arrangements to bury my beloved husband the following Saturday after his death. It is a funny thing mothers and daughters, our relationships are often complicated. We love fiercely, and we fight fiercely. As we prepared to bury her father, my beloved husband, I figured that we would fight about what he would wear, the size and style of his casket, or which tie to rest on his stately neck. I would stand my ground and we would battle for days. I knew I raised a strong woman in Corinne and her way was generally the one that we all followed. Corinne had an inner strength and relentless determination that was hard to shake. Our usual cadence didn't occur this time though. This time, I let her win because I had no more fight in me. It was not that I was weak, I was exhausted. In this season of my life, I just did not have any fight left. I figured it did not matter what he wore or the box that would be covered in dirt. So why argue about it? None of it was important to me. I wanted Sam to rest in peace because he had fought for so long and he had earned it.

The morning of his funeral I asked that only Nia accompany me in the limousine. I did not want the entire family with me, because I did not want to be fussed over. I just wanted to be myself and grieve in my own way.

My daughter was a successful newscaster for our local ABC station, *WBRD*. She was constantly busy building her career and didn't notice the unrelenting toll that Cancer had taken on her father and me. I had lived with and cared for him for 4 years, so his death wasn't a complete surprise. I saw Cancer eat away at him physically and mentally, everyday. Its affects were metastatic. Corrine was doing everything she could to atone for her absence during his illness and fussing over me was going to be another way for her to heal. It was too late. I was sick with grief, and I didn't want her to turn me into a patient. Also, I thought that I was fine. It was hard for the family to understand that I had buried my husband years ago. He was physically there, but his spirit died long before that morning in the hospital. I lost his mind soon after, and his boyishness, decades before that. Joy hadn't visited our home in years. We were merely occupying the same space and engaging in occasional conversation. I often spoke to Nia about what was going on. She would wave off the sadness and change the subject to something related to me, not Sam's illness. She had walked this journey with me and she understood my pain. Because of that, I knew that she was the only one that would treat me like a normal person, not like a fragile, wounded widow.

There was something special about my granddaughter. She was our only. Nia was a free spirit and did not allow anyone to dictate her life, including her mother. Corinne and James had always kept Nia in a box. She was required to do and be everything that they wanted. She had to run in the right circles, and go to the right schools, and participate in the right activities. But Nia was never one to subscribe to their agenda. She marched to the beat of her own drum. And I love that about her. Part of me thinks that she would does things just to annoy her mother. This service was no exception. Walking to the limo, I noticed that she was wearing a hot-pink jumpsuit to her grandfather's funeral. The storm would rage with Corrine's disdain as soon as Nia walked up to the car. Before she was close, I heard Corrine's screeching.

"How could you wear THAT to your grandfather's funeral? And those heels! My God Nia you are going to sink into the grass at the cemetery. Couldn't you just have worn something more modest? Flats at least?"

In her own way, Nia dismissed the comments. She kissed her mother on the forehead and slid into the limousine with me. As Corrine was still ridiculing Nia's fashion choice, she closed the door of the car to muffle her mothers voice. She looked at me and said, "That's yo' daughter!" I laughed a bit as I watched Nia slide on a pair of black over-sized sunglasses and cross her long legs at the ankle.

The service was short and dignified, just the way Sam would have wanted it. Traditional hymns were sung, and standard scripture passages were recited. Our church, Bethel Baptist, had been our spiritual home for over 30 years. Pastor Rawls has been there for the last fifteen, and he'd become a close personal friend of both Sam and I. He was a young man, tall, heavy, and a passionate preacher who knew the Word of God inside and out. At the end of the services, he offered his condolences to me and my family as he committed my husband into the earth at the adjoining cemetery. Six generations of our family were buried there and now, my husband Sam would join them.

I requested that there not be a repast after the funeral. I wanted to go home. I was tired, and I didn't need one more ounce of church punch, store bought potato salad, canned green beans, brick-like macaroni and cheese, a cold roll, or *Costco* rotisserie chicken. I didn't need the church mothers and hospitality committee to visit or "comfort" me. I didn't want the deacons to offer another prayer, and had no need to become a member of the widow's ministry group. The hustle and bustle of funerals and dealing with the depth of my loss was exhausting, both spiritually and physically. There was no need for me to have additional food brought to the house, as my church and club members had outfitted me with enough food to feed an army for a month. No. I just wanted to be left alone to feel this new normal. I didn't need to be eased into it. I wanted to feel it all at once. I figured that the faster I get into my new normal, the better I would feel. Ignoring my cues, Corinne asked if I wanted her to stay with me.

"Mom, you really shouldn't be alone. I'll drop James off and come spend the night. He has to be at work early to prepare for that deposition and I need to make sure you're OK."

I looked into the eyes of my only child, grasped her two hands and said, "Corrine, I'm fine. Go home. You and James go have dinner and get a good night's sleep. You have done a lot and you need to rest, and James needs to get ready for tomorrow. I'm going to be fine." Begrudgingly, Corrine left.

"I'm just a phone call away, mom."

"I know."

Corrine grabbed her purse, kissed my cheek, and left.

The door slammed shut and I realized, instantly, that I wasn't fine. I needed someone at the house with me, but Corrine was a worry wart, and she would not be a calming force. She would spend her time asking if I was OK, or if I needed more tea or a pillow fluffed. In her own way, she would have thought doting over me would be helpful, but it would have done more harm than good. The last thing I wanted was to be fussed over and that is exactly what Corrine would have done. I didn't want to sit and grieve. I wanted to be distracted and take my mind off the vortex of sadness and loss that swirled around me. I knew that Nia was coming over later in the evening to talk about life and dine on pizza and champagne. Nia has always been a sounding board for me, even as a small child.

She was born to Corrine and James after a hard fight of infertility. Corrine had struggled for years. My daughter was never in great health, but after high school, she decided to take a more holistic approach to dealing with her asthma. She became a vegetarian and started swimming daily. She had taken corticosteroids for decades to help her breathe. When it came time for she and James to start a family, she discovered that her uterus was overtaken by massive fibroid tumors, making it difficult, if not impossible, to carry a baby to term. She always attributed her infertility to the asthma treatments and all the drugs that she was prescribed to help her breathe, but there was no scientific evidence to prove it. She needed something or someone to blame for the infertility and the subsequent sense of inadequacy.

She became pregnant with Nia after two miscarriages. The doctor immediately put her on bed rest for six months while Nia grew in her already crowded womb. Nia was our miracle baby. Corinne had almost given up the hope of having a child. She and James had gone on a month-long vacation to Hawaii after their last round of IVF, to get their minds off all of the treatments that they had endured and medication that Corinne had been taking. Six weeks later, Corinne announced that she was pregnant. We held our collective breath for months. We had gone through this before, only to be left with no baby. Each time she miscarried, a seed of sadness and anger was planted in Corinne's already broken heart. The loss of a child almost killed her physically and it paralyzed her mentally. My once fun-loving daughter was reduced to a bitter, angry, resentful woman. It was understandable. Although I had never experienced anything close to what Corinne experienced, I understood how anger is the harvest after the seed of loss is sown.

After a final round of IVF, Nia came into the world at 5 pounds 7 ounces, 22 inches long. She was beautiful. She reminded me so much of her mother when she was born. And now, just like every other parent, Corinne watched as Nia became her own person. They always dreamed that Nia would become the next Oprah. She would sit, mesmerized in front of the TV after school, watching Oprah conduct interviews. She even had her own show where she would interview her stuffed animals, while her dolls served as audience members. Corinne beamed with pride and had such hope for Nia's future. She often brought Nia to the set of the station and envisioned a future mother/daughter broadcast team. She was so outgoing, that they believed that it was the beginning of her career in broadcast journalism.

Even as an infant, Nia's personality was infectious. Corinne was so protective of Nia when she was a child, and even now, as an adult.

She was enrolled in a dance class when she was 6, and promptly decided that choreography was not for her. At her first recital, instead of performing the prescribed moves, she broke out into a freestyle routine that sent the audience into a frenzy. Corinne and James were mortified. It was Nia's first introduction to breaking the mold and making the rules for herself. Then and now, she lives her life on her own terms. When it was time for Nia to go to college, she rebuffed her parents by attending a historical Black college. Corinne and James had met at the University of Michigan. Nia, however, decided that she was not going to a predominantly White institution. She had always had her heart set on attending Hampton University in Virginia. There was something about that domed chapel and lakeside campus that intrigued her, even though her parents objected. She decided that she would pursue exercise science, which again caused Corinne and James to stand up on end. She had different plans for her future.

"How in the world are you supposed to make a living studying exercise?" Corrine asked. "I mean you're not Jane Fonda and anybody can exercise. I'm spending my money to send you to college so that you can learn how to do push ups?"

Corinne always said that a degree in exercise science was useless, and that Nia had wasted her time and money studying foolishness. Nia stood her ground and found a way to pay for college all by herself because her parents decided to spend her college fund on a vacation home in Martha's Vineyard after they pulled their support for her education during her freshman year. That was the price to pay for not selecting a degree that her parents approved of. I thought that Corrine and James were too harsh. I suppose it was my fault since I raised Corrine to stand up for her beliefs, and not accept anything less than the best. I certainly didn't think that she would take her stance this far, against the interest of her daughter, but she did.

The limousine dropped me off at my house at about 5:00 in the afternoon. The funeral attendant walked me to my door and offered a somber goodbye.

Holding my hand he said, "On behalf of everyone at Blessed Rest Funeral Home, I offer our sincere condolences. May the peace of God be with you during this time of bereavement."

His face was down turned and his gait was solemn as he walked away. I looked down at my hand that was just embraced by his, and there lay a business card, *Blessed Rest and Nothing Less*. I laughed a bit to myself. Blessed Rest was marketing even at that moment. As I walked into the door, I felt the stagnation of the air. There was no one to greet me. Sam was gone, and I was alone. I forbade the family from coming home with me. Even Nia. I wanted to experience the sadness of being alone, and there was no sense prolonging the inevitable. Plus, having people at the house would require me to talk as they offered their sympathies.

"He was a good man."

"You were blessed to have him for as long as you did."

"To be absent from the body is to be present with the Lord."

I didn't want to hear any of it. I just wanted my husband back.

I kicked off my shoes that had long pinched my toes to numbness and flopped into Sam's favorite chair where I soon curled up in his blanket and wept. Why him? He was a lovely man and a wonderful father. He suffered for so long and I never heard him complain once. I loved him and I know he loved me. The glow of the television seeped into the room, and it shone like moonlight. I peeled myself from the chair to finally take off my funeral clothes. I needed and wanted a hot shower. As the warm water ran over my naked body, I spotted his bath gel and loofah. I decided I would wash my body with his things. I thought, just for an instant, I would be able to feel him on me again. The gelatinous bath wash foamed up and the suds fell all over my skin. The roughness of the loofah seemed to scrub away the day's events. I stayed in the shower until the water ran cold, and I stepped out on to the soft microfiber rug. I never used a towel to dry off. Instead, I preserved my brown skin by just applying coconut oil while I was still wet.

People have always marveled at the beauty of my flawless skin. It is remarkably golden bronze and taut. When my age had crept in, my skin made no transition. I look a lot younger than my 73 years suggests. I credit it to lots of water, good living, a positive attitude, and coconut oil. Sam always loved it and had no problem when I would wear clothes that revealed just a little more skin than most women my age would be comfortable with showing. Just as I was finishing up my left leg, I heard the doorbell and then a key. Nia was here.

"Gram? I'm here. I brought pizza and I figured instead of champagne it felt more like a beer night...what do you think?"

I emerged from my bathroom in a sweat suit that Nia had gotten me. It was soft like cotton inside, warm, and over-sized. It was the perfect thing to wear for a pizza and beer night with my granddaughter.

"I'm glad you brought beer. Champagne feels like a celebration, and today was not a day to celebrate."

My granddaughter and I sat on the floor crying and reminiscing about Sam as we chomped on pepperoni pizza and three bottles of

Stella Artois beer, each.

Our discussion soon turned to what was going on in Nia's life, which was fine by me. I didn't want to talk about Sam anymore. That evening, I talked myself till I was blue in the face about our life, and how he died and how I would miss him so much. I did not want to talk about that anymore. Nia told me all about her acceptance into graduate school. She had done it in secret so that her mother would not have anything to say about it. Corrine had always wanted Nia to get a master's or law degree, but in exercise science? I didn't even think that was possible. But Nia, ever the optimist, found a program that fit exactly what she wanted to do.

"So Gram, what I'm going to do is get a masters in kinesiology. That way I can open up my gym or I can be a trainer for stars, or I can be a trainer for professional athletes, or I can be a fitness trainer, or I could train other trainers…"

She went on and on about what her desires and aspirations were in this field of fitness. I had never been particularly active, so all the things she was talking about were completely foreign to me. I smiled, encouraged her, and told her that she can do anything she set her mind to. I believe in her.

"Nia, what I know about you, sweetheart, is that you can do anything, and I mean anything, you want to do. You always have. You have never allowed yourself to succumb to the will or the whims of other people. Don't you dare start doing that now. Live your life well and free. It goes by really fast."

I knew the swiftness of life all too well. Fifty years had gone by in a flash. I looked up and I was married with a child. Then, seconds later, my daughter was grown with a child of her own, then, my Sam was gone. It was over before it started.

Nia quickly changed the subject from her schooling to her love life. I wasn't so naïve to think that my 26 year-old granddaughter was a virgin. I assumed that she had had one or two sexual experiences in high school, or most certainly, in college since she had been dating Bryce, her college sweetheart. She and Bryce had met the first semester of her freshman year and they were on and off for the entire four years of her matriculation. He was tall and handsome and came from the exact type of family that Corrine wanted Nia to marry into. Bryce's family owned a string of car dealerships in Douglasville, a small suburb of Atlanta. Their relationship was rocky from the start.

From what I could decipher from our many conversations, Nia looked the part of a potential wife for Bryce, but he didn't like her "wild ways." He tried to control her free-spirit and it was always a point of contention. Corrine wanted Bryce and Nia to be a couple. She loved the idea that Nia would be a member of a prestigious family and wouldn't want for anything. Nia, however, had other plans. When they finally decided to breakup five days after graduation, Corrine called Bryce and begged him to take Nia back. Nia was livid. She went to her parents' home and confronted Corrine with such anger, James had to intervene. I learned of the falling out from Corrine and she, as always, didn't feel like she had done anything wrong.

"Momma, she is ruining her life! I was just trying to help her secure her future." Her logic was well-intended but her methods, I thought, were horrible.

As usual, I said nothing about how I felt about the situation and instead, I offered a, "Well, just pray about it, sweetheart." I wanted to scream at the top of my lungs! Corrine wanted to control everyone's life but her own. Where had I failed her as a mother?

Nia talked for an hour and described a warm sun-soaked world full of new words, new activities, and new questions that I needed answers to. She closed her eyes and stretched her long lithe legs, doing, what I assumed was a yoga pose. She rose in one elegant motion, took a deep, unrestrained breath, and bent deeply at the waist while bringing her knees into her chest. I watched and listened. How I wish I could be so free and unrestrained like her.

She breathed in an even deeper breath, "Sensual yoga class, Gram. It's amazing," she said while she pulled her arms over head and crossed them palm-to-palm. By now, she had performed her contortions and Nia sat crossed legged on the whiskey leather ottoman.

"Gram, it's freed me! It's hot yoga but instead of focusing on stretching our limbs, we meditate and nurture our erogenous zones."

I sat attentively and acted like I understood what she was saying.

"You have no idea what I'm talking about do you Gram?" I think Nia could see my confusion which I attempted to mask with subtle nods and soft "OKs" as she spoke.

"We didn't talk about that stuff in my day. We didn't get to talk about our feelings either." I looked into the eyes of my granddaughter and for the first time I saw a look that spoke volumes. It was pity. Her blank expression revealed her secret -- she felt sorry for me. Nia scooted closer to me and took my hands in hers.

"Gram?"

I turned away from her, feeling ashamed and embarrassed. I had lived three times as long as Nia, yet there was still so much for me to learn about being a woman.

When Sam got sick, every time Nia came to our house, she would sleep on the floor next to us. It never seemed strange that she wanted to be close. When she was a little girl, she would climb in our bed and snuggle between us and burrow her head in a fluffy pillow. She was a wild sleeper and our rest, in those days, was limited when she spent the night. We would watch her sleep and when she was settled in, we would move her onto a pallet that we made on the floor. From that point, she always slept on the floor in our room. True to form, Nia gathered up the softest blanket in the house and curled herself up in the fetal position at the foot of our bed.

I climbed in on the right side leaving the left side completely intact and whispered, "Nia? Tomorrow we have to get rid of this bed."

"I got you Gram. I will call Orlando and Enid tomorrow to have them come and help. Don't worry, it will be gone by tomorrow night."

2

The Day After the Night Before

The next morning, I woke up before Nia. I had to step over her to go to the bathroom, and as I looked down at her sweet golden face, I saw that little girl that I watched enter the world 26 years earlier. She is a beautiful woman, but in my eyes, she was still my grandchild who toddled all through our home. She had not changed one bit. She was so happy-go-lucky as a child, and that wonder and joy hadn't faded at all. She has always been independent and strong, and I admire that. Stepping over her, trying desperately not to wake her up, I tip toed into the bathroom. My bare feet hit the tile floor and the coolness of the travertine jolted me into an even more conscious state.

I looked at myself in the mirror and thought:

Here I am. A widow. A 73 year-old widow.

I looked tired, and my skin didn't have its usual bronze glow. It was dry and had a gray hue that made me look…well…old. That's how I saw myself now. I am an old widow. I wondered if that was how the world would see me too. If I would be defined by his death. Would my life be forever changed because now, I was not married, but rather, I was a widow?

It seemed unfair that Sam had so much freedom in his death. That he was finally able to be all that he wanted to be with no obligation or responsibility. I imagined him soaring through the sky laughing and doing things he never thought he could do or would be physically able to do. I was jealous of his freedom. I was still down here, but now, alone, defined only by the death of my husband. All the business of his death still had to be handled. Removing his name from the bank account, turning off his cell phone, informing the Postal Service that he was no longer alive, obtaining a death certificate, receiving insurance payouts, paying off credit card bills, and all the other things that death causes those that live to have to endure. That person, that shell that lay in that hospital bed, was not my husband. His spirit had died four years before when he was diagnosed with Lung Cancer.

He stopped being himself the moment Dr. Swain spoke those words. We sat in his office that was painted with his undergraduate degree from Howard University and his medical degree from Meharry Medical College. Peppered in between were certificates, commendations, and awards from his beloved Alpha Phi Alpha Fraternity, Incorporated, John's Hopkins University, City of Hope, and several others. I remember holding Sam's hand tight as we sat in the wooden chairs across from Dr. Swain. He was an older Black doctor, renowned for his Cancer treatments and research efforts, as well as his advocacy in the city for communities that lacked access to medical care. He was a pillar in Hilbrand and his knowledge of innovative Cancer treatments was revolutionary.

"Mr. Ashworth, Mrs. Ashworth, it's Cancer. Stage 4 Lung Cancer. I'm so sorry."

We sat stunned and then he said, "I think the best course of action is several aggressive rounds of chemotherapy and radiation, but I must tell you that stage 4 means that it has metastasized."

He talked for an hour. I remember little of what he said. Our empty stare must have made Dr. Swain uncomfortable because he waited in silence with us as we processed the information that changed the entire course of our lives.

Almost immediately, Sam began to decline. The next morning, when he woke, he was already different. He seemed older and weak. I believe that after his diagnosis, he decided that instead of fighting, he would rather prepare to die. My role changed too. I went from wife to caretaker in 24 hours. Our vows were playing out in real time. His breathing became more labored, and his activity became more stifled. He stopped being my husband, and was now my patient.

I tended to every need that he had because that was what I was required to do as his wife. I hated it. I dare not say that out loud, but I hated not having a husband. I was angry at him and furious with Cancer. Both robbed me of my Sam. I know it sounds selfish, but we were just about to begin our life together and, in an instant, our dreams were dashed. People think that life ends after 70, but I believed that ours was just beginning. We had gone through childrearing and career building. Our house was paid off, and our life was comfortable. We had trips planned and our morning coffee dates to the Coffee Haus were a daily occurrence. We were having fun, and then, Cancer barged in, decimated our present, and ruined our future.

I was even looking forward to having a more intimate relationship with Sam. I had read on the Internet that men and women in their 70s had very active sex lives. Sam and I had always had a deep and loving connection, but sex was not high on our list of priorities. We had not really been sexually active in years. We had a traditional mindset that sex was utility. It was a means to produce children, not to necessarily enjoy. Those days had long past, and we were content sleeping in the same bed with no room for sex or passion. A few years ago, we had gone to a Sex After 70 workshop at the senior center by accident. We thought that the topic was going to be about preventing Gout. Instead, we sat through a two-hour workshop on how sex aids in heart health and learned tips for practicing safe sex for seniors. The speaker, a sex therapist, told the group that seniors that have sex on a regular basis are healthier and happier.

"Sign me up!" Sam said eagerly. The audience erupted in laughter.

My cheeks were hot with embarrassment, and I giggled nervously during the entire session. By the end of the night, we had learned so much and it felt like life had given us permission to live again. Sam and I left that meeting inspired to explore our newfound sex life. The idea was short-lived as his diagnosis came just a week later. The truth of the matter is that though we slept in the same bed, we had not touched each other intimately in a decade or more. I did not think anything strange about it either. We were, after all, in our 70s, and who thinks about intimacy in their 70s?

Marriage at that point is all about caring and helpfulness. When you are with someone for 50 years, you stop being married around year 32 and you end up being partners, or roommates, or caretakers of one another. Our marriage was wonderful and beautiful and produced our daughter, but it certainly was not an intimate one. There was no tenderness at all. Especially after the diagnosis. Our love was Agape love, there were no Cupid's arrows or Eros. It was routine and benign. The therapist said that passion had to be cultivated and that many couples get comfortable and hang up their sex lives when they get old. She told us to be more Blanche and less Dorothy! It is not that I have any resentment, but it is hard to feel intimate with your husband when you are having to wipe up his sputum from the floor or accompany him to the bathroom. It changes the dynamic of your relationship.

As I sat watching and looking at myself in the mirror, I wondered whether I would ever be the same. How my life would change, if at all. I wondered if I would ever have life again. And if I did, what would it be? I felt like I would never know joy again. I knew that factually. In my soul I believed that joy left me when Sam took his last breath. I would live out the rest of my days, just puttering around the house, or being an obedient parent to my child, and a soft place to fall for my granddaughter. My role as wife was done, my role as a woman was done, and I was left only to be of service to those who were still here with me.

As promised, Enid and Orlando, came over to remove the mattress, bedframe and headboard from me and Sam's bedroom. The three of them hauled it away in a U-Haul truck that Orlando rented for the day. Nia told me that she was going to donate the bedroom set to a shelter in a neighboring city. I was heartbroken and relieved as I watched the bed that Sam and I slept in, roll away in a dirty moving truck. I tossed the sheets and mattress pad in the recycle bin in the alley of our home and turned away to cry.

When someone dies you tend to put things into perspective. Priorities shift. Those sheets had been washed on the delicate cycle 20 times and I took time to iron them if they came out too wrinkled. Now, they lined the trashcan in our alley, all because I couldn't bear to sleep on them. Even after a wash, they smelled like Sam. In return, Nia bought me the most beautiful Posturepedic bed. It was so comfortable, and it was mine. We had always had a California king size bed, but, this time, she bought me a queen size bed. She said, "Gram, a queen bed for a queen." I appreciated her gesture. Having a large bed was just too much and would remind me that I was in it by myself. Nia always thought of the most wonderful things. She knew me and what my needs were. Corrine had come over to help me make the bed with the new bed sheets and bedspread. Pure white. Pure white bed sheets and a pure white comforter. Corrine had suggested, years ago, to have all our bedding and towels in pure white. I thought it was a bad idea, then I discovered the ease of bleaching everything. Sold! I continued the tradition. It felt and looked like sleeping on a cloud. I couldn't wait to hop into it every night. I dug myself into the soft billows of the mattress and covered up with the marshmallow-like comforter on hot and cool evenings. The pillows were made with bamboo fibers and my head sunk right into them. My bed felt like a hug from my beloved Sam. But it was my bed. A queen for queen.

For the next six months, I saw Nia every day. She came over to my house to visit and do her best to pry me out of the stupor that I found myself in. This day, Nia had come over to discuss all her new adventures in graduate school. Again, I pretended like I understood. I didn't. I had decided to tell Nia that I no longer needed her to come over as frequently to keep me company. I was fine, or at least, that's what I wanted her to believe. The truth was, I wanted to be alone and wallow in my own sadness. Having her visit reminded me that I needed to figure out a way to stand on my own without Sam here.

"Gram what are you going to do all day?" Nia asked.

I had no idea. I had spent the last six months watching the *Price Is Right* every morning, and *Judge Judy* every afternoon. In between, I enjoyed having lunch by myself in the kitchen while playing *Candy Crush* on my cell phone and preparing dinner for one. My nights were spent watching *Family Feud*, taking a shower, moisturizing my body with coconut oil, and going to bed, just to do it all over again the next day. I had become a master of routine. I had no activities, and I certainly didn't want them at this point. What was I going to do, go to some bridge club? I didn't even play bridge. I am 73 years old, and I had no desire to do anything except wait to die. My family would offer to babysit me and include me in their family outings. I had no interest. It always felt as though I was a third wheel during those family trips. I felt like a charity case. I know my family loves me, but I also know that they invited me to things out of a sense of obligation or fear that I would be by myself. It was safe for me to be an island. I could process my feelings and think about things and cry and weep and grieve without any judgment or question. It was OK that Corrine, James, and Nia had moved on with their lives and that they had activity and purpose. And it was also OK that I did not. I didn't realize how much of those four years were taken up with just caring for Sam. I had taken such good care of him, that I had neglected myself. And I didn't know how to do that now, so I just decided I wouldn't.

Nia objected to my decision not to have her come over every

day. She never takes no for an answer.

"Gram, I'll be here tomorrow. I don't care what you have to say. I'm coming over because if I don't come over here, then I'll be with Corrine, and you know that's not going to work."

I understood. Nia lives in the guest house that was located on the grounds where Corinne and James had their large home. Their living situation was like mixing oil and water in the middle of a nuclear power plant. That house could blow at any time. They could not get along, not because they did not love each other, but because Nia had no desire to compromise and neither did Corinne. James often sat quietly shaking his head or reading a book paying no attention to either of them.

"Nia seriously, it's OK. I don't need you to come every day, sweetheart. But if you want to come, to get away from your mother, I understand. What time shall I expect you?"

"I'll be there at 9:00 in the morning."

When she was at the house, she always opened her books and her laptop and spread them out like a mosaic on the floor. I would bring her chamomile tea and watch *Family Feud* on mute, struggling to read the lips of Steve Harvey and the eager contestants. She would mention things like torque and muscle groups, posterior and anterior whatchamacallits, and other technical terms that I didn't understand. But as she studied, I saw her fill up with joy. She loved the human body and how it could do so many wonderful things. She was truly in her element in this master's program, and I wished that Corinne could support her in it. But, she didn't.

3

Cleaning Out

People underestimate the gravity of the death of a spouse. I thought that burying Sam would be the hardest thing that I had to deal with. I was wrong. I had endured the funeral and the days, weeks, and months following his death, but my hardest days were coming. I spent the better part of my time puttering around the house and finding menial tasks to fill the hours of the day. Walking through the house meant dealing with the constant reminders of my husband, and the life that we shared for over 50 years. Seeing his clothes in the closet, his favorite cup in the kitchen cabinet, or his slippers under the bed, caused me tremendous sadness, but more than anything, I saw the past living in my present. I was drowning, but I felt guilty for feeling that way. I had no way of knowing what was next for me, but I knew I wanted to be free from the burden of my yesterday.

I woke up on Tuesday, May 16, early in the morning, after a deep and wonderful rest. I had gone to bed around 8:00 PM the night before, and I arose with the sun. I clicked on the light on my nightstand. The clock read 6:18 AM. Staring at the ceiling, I began to silently cry. Grief is a crazy thing. They say that there are stages that you go through when a loved one dies or tragedy strikes -- denial, anger, bargaining, depression, and acceptance. I had no idea what stage I was in. I suppose, to a certain extent, I was feeling all of them at the same time. I was angry one moment, and accepting of the fact that he was gone the next. Laying in the bed that morning, I was feeling tired. Even after a long, restful night, I was exhausted. Sam was gone, but he was still here. Everything about him was here. His clothes, his shoes, his energy, his smell, his medical equipment. Everything was still here. Each item, a reminder of what I had lost, not of what I had for the past 50 years, 4 months, and 27 days. Those things lived in my heart. Fifty years weren't housed in the things of life, rather, those 50 years were in the marrow of my being. I decided, that day, to rid myself and the house of his things. As I was contemplating how to attack his closet, the phone rang.

"Hey mom." Corrine's voice rang in my ear like a well-tuned bell.

"Hi dear. What are you up to and why are you up so early?" I responded trying not to sound like what I was feeling.

"I covered Vanessa's 4:00 AM broadcast. I just got off the air from my 6:00 AM show, and I was thinking about coming over today. Are you busy?" Corrine knew that I watched her 6:00 AM broadcast every morning. I loved seeing her face on the local news. As the anchor, she led the rest of the cast every morning. She was beautiful and poised. Her skills had been honed during her time at the University of Michigan and during her years of on-air experience in Hilbrand, and in nearby Nelford, covering tragedies to triumphs.

I thought for a minute. Should I let her come over *today?*

"Uh, no, I'm not busy but I was going to…" Before I could finish my sentence, Corrine responded eagerly.

"Great. I'll see you at ten. Love you." Then the phone clicked.

I sat straight up in my bed. *Well, this is going to be interesting.* I was not going to be deterred from my plan to clean out Sam's things just because Corrine was coming over. I knew that it was going to be a battle, but I needed to do this so that I could be free from the daily reminder of my loss.

I eased out of bed and shuffled to the bathroom. The splash of cold water that hit my face after my routine of cleansing and exfoliation, was all the motivation I needed to wake all the way up. I finished my routine with a creamy, all-natural moisturizer and coconut oil, that I layered on my face and neck. I walked past Sam's closet before getting to my own. His clothes remained in perfect form. His militaristic ways were ever-present as his clothes and shoes were lined up like they were preparing for drills. I reached my closet, that was organized, but not nearly as neat as Sam's. A slate gray sweat suit was my uniform for the day. I grabbed a bottle of water and a box of black trash bags from the kitchen and made my way back to the bedroom. Standing in Sam's closet, I said a silent prayer.

Dear God, give me strength. Amen.

I started with his shirts. Color coordinated and organized by sleeve length, I reached in and released each one from its wooden hanger. Plaid, button-down, polo, short-sleeved, flannel, silk, linen, cotton. Every shirt held a memory and I took the time to savor each one. As the memory solidified in my mind, I gently placed the shirt in the black bag. I thought that I was going to feel sad as I bagged Sam's clothes, but with each item, I was lifted. My spirit became lighter and more free. I realized that my memories were in my mind and heart, not in fabric, buttons, or pigment. When I finally reached the white shirts, I found the one that I dreaded locating — Perry Ellis, white, button-down shirt with the small pale-blue buttons. This was the shirt that he wore the day that he was diagnosed. He hadn't worn it since then. I wouldn't allow it. I never wanted to see that shirt again. It was the uniform that he wore to his greatest and most difficult battle. It was his war shirt. I hated it. I tore it from the hanger and did my best to rip it into shreds. What started as me pulling off buttons, turned into me tearing the shirt into pieces with reckless abandon. I was free. The destruction of that shirt, the feeling of tearing it, freed me from the confines of Sam's Cancer. The fabric of my life had been torn and I needed to rid myself from the ties that bound me to my new definition.

I heard the door open. "Mommmmmm....? It's me?" Corrine yelled from the family room. I had filled three black bags with Sam's clothing.

"I was thinking that we should go to lunch and then hit the mall. What do you think?" Corrine's voice was nearing, and my heart began to race. I knew what her reaction was going to be.

"Mom?"

"Yeah honey, I'm in the bedroom." I called back.

Corrine rounded the corner and stopped mid-sentence. "What are you doing, momma?"

"Cleaning out."

Corrine walked slowly toward the now, almost empty closet. She turned in a circle, searching for an answer on the empty racks. I kept working, moving bags out and removing shoes, belts, and sweaters.

"Stop it momma!" Corrine yelled as fury filled her eyes. "Stop it now!"

I looked up at her and she was seething mad.

"What are you doing? This is daddy's stuff, and you..." She was breathless. Her chest was heaving and her eyes were filled with tears.

"I can't believe you!" Corrine stormed out of the room and before I could respond, the front door slammed shut. My freedom, it seemed, came with a cost. My daughter was in a rage while I was finding peace. I wondered which I should tend to first. A mother typically tends to the needs of her children before she tends to her own. But this time, I took care of myself. It was a first. It felt selfish and self-centered, but I maintained my stance. For once, I was going to live for me, and nothing was going to stop me — not even my daughter.

The 19 black trash bags filled the family room. Sitting in Sam's whiskey leather easy chair, I stared at his belongings. There, in those bags, were 50 years of of his stuff. In those bags where birthday parties and cotillions, Monday Night Football and Must-See TV. His pajamas, his tuxedo, his ties, and his tennis shoes. All of them were packed in bags ready to be donated to a needy organization. It's what he would have wanted. I did keep some things that I thought Corrine or Nia would want. His gold watch that he received after retiring from Houghton, his wedding band, his rosary, his handkerchief that he tucked in his breast pocket when he walked Corrine down the aisle when she married James, the orange and blue tie that he wore when Nia graduated from Hampton, and a pair of his favorite Nike Pegasus sneakers. I didn't keep anything for myself. Everything that I wanted, I already had, in my mind and in my heart. The material items held no value to me. If I couldn't have Sam, then I didn't want anything. My marriage was over and I was beginning to think that my life was too, and no *thing* was going to make that better.

4

No Rest for the Weary

When the last load of clothing was loaded into the back of Orlando's SUV, Nia and I stood in the door way, speechless. I wasn't sad. I felt lost. I think that's why so many people have a hard time getting rid of a deceased loved one's clothing. It seems so final. It is the realization that they aren't coming back. It's terrible, actually. Leaving their things in tact reminds you that they aren't there. Getting rid of it reminds you that they are never coming back. It is the ultimate conundrum. For me, I needed to let the physical items go. It was time. It was beyond time. Nia wrapped her arms around me and guided me into the house as Orlando drove away.

I was sitting on the sofa when Nia came in with a tray that held 2 cups, a teapot, and a saucer of limes. She poured a small amount of liquid into each cup and grabbed a lime. "Fuck tea. You need Tequila." Nia said as she toasted the air and took a shot. She winced as she squeezed the lime between her perfectly white teeth. I followed suit. Yep, Tequila was exactly what I needed.

"Hey," Nia said mid-shot, "let's have a slumber party tonight."

"A what?" I asked as my sober mind began to cloud.

"A slumber party. Imma call Enid, Hailey, Livy, and Shell to come over. Oh...and Orlando can come back too. It'll be fun, Gram."

I was apprehensive. An evening with a gaggle of Millennials? *What on earth would we talk about?*

"I have no problem with you and your friends coming over. I'll stay in the bedroom and you guys can have the run of the house."

"No, Gram. We're going to dish and spill some tea! You gotta be in the mix." Nia said with glee. She was reaching for her phone to send a group text to her crew.

"Spill tea? Dish? I don't get it. Should I bring out more teacups?" I asked naively.

"No Gram." Nia chuckled and shook her head. "We are going to talk, eat, and drink. These types of nights we talk about everything from politics to IG filters, from yoga to best positions to achieve the best orgasms."

I blushed. "Yeah...this seems like I would be out of my element. I'll leave you all to it." I tried getting up, but the Tequila shot harnessed me to the ground.

"Gram, you're gonna be fine. I promise." Nia reassured me, "We will take it easy. I promise."

Her phone sang like a symphony. *Bing. Bing. Bing.* With every notification, Nia yelled out a hearty, "Yassss."

I sat on the floor with my back resting against the ottoman. "Why are we so excited?"

"Everybody will be here at 7:00 PM." Nia popped up and began dancing around the house. "Owwww...yasss..." Nia started playing music from her phone.

I'm a savage.

Classy.

Bougie.

Ratchet.

She was shaking her body into a frenzy.

"Come on Gram!" she yelled. "Let's get it."

I'm a savage.

I peeled myself off the floor and started to move my hips. I hadn't danced in years. The last time I had danced was at Corrine and James' wedding, almost 30 years ago. We had danced a choreographed number at our 50th anniversary party, but Sam was sick and the "dance" was more of a series of slow sways, with me holding him up and faking an endearing smile, like it was normal. For us, it was *our* normal.

Dancing with Nia, however, wasn't a waltz or a series of awkward sways and fake smiles. She was using her legs and her hips to pop to the rhythm of Megan The Stallion. Her head was cocked to the side, her knees bent, and her bottom was gyrating in a way that mesmerized even me.

"Come on Gram. Shake it!!"

I mimicked her motion and did my best to move in the way that she did. She laughed and fell out onto the sofa in uncontrollable laughter.

"Gram you were gettin' it!" Nia said, as she took a third shot of Tequila.

"I don't know about that, but I'm damn sure feelin' it!" I said as I grabbed my hip.

A few hours later, after a well deserved nap, after way too much Tequila and not enough food, we were shaken into consciousness when the doorbell rang. Nia stumbled to the door.

"Heyyyyyyy…" She yelled. I heard a sea of chatter from Shell, Enid, Hailey, and Livy.

"We hangin' with Gram tonight. Where she at?" Livy said loudly with her signature Southern drawl. "Gram…where you at?"

The swarm entered the family room, each with a bottle in hand, holding a slew of designer bags. Prada, Louis Vuitton, Michael Kors, and Gucci symbols flooded my family room. Each of Nia's friends had been to our home a million times. Nia grew up with Shell, Hailey, and Livy, but Enid and Orlando were friends that she met while matriculating at Hampton. Orlando was the lone male in the group. He had a girlfriend who was understanding of his relationship with all of the women in his life. He tolerated the chatter and silliness of the girls, and although he and Nia had once dated, he remained part of their gaggle of girlfriends.

"Where's Do?" Hailey asked as she hugged me. "Hey Gram. How you been?"

"I've been doing the best I can, sweetness." I responded.

The girls settled down in the family room, claiming their respective spots on the sofa and the floor. They seated me in Sam's chair. They coined it the "Wisdom Chair" for the evening. I was to be the voice of reason and information to this group of extremely accomplished young women. Each was educated and all were successful in their chosen professions. Livy was a vice principal at a middle school in Nelford, Hailey was a dentist, Shell owned a day spa, and Enid was a federal prosecutor. Orlando loved cars and was a custom car designer. My Nia, after completing her master's degree, was determined to open a gym.

"So, y'all," Nia stated as she stood in the middle of the room holding an open bottle of wine, "Tonight, we are holding court. This night is all about Gram." The girls looked my way. I bowed my head in confusion. "We are celebrating her tonight! She is getting her life and we are here to support her and love her through it." The girls began snapping their fingers like they were at an open mic night at a spoken word bar. Nia had given the bottle to Shell and she began pouring small shots for everyone. Nia stood next to me, and put her hand on my shoulder. "So, here's to Gram and her new normal. Rest well to my Pop-Pop and now it's time to awaken my Gram. To Gram." We raised our glasses, and the girls took their shots. I chose to fake it. One more glass of Tequila would have sent me over the edge, free falling into unconsciousness.

"So Gram, I got a question," Shell asked. "What's it like? You know…marriage for 50 years?"

I didn't know how to answer her question. *What was it like?* I started thinking about my life with Sam and I got lost in my thoughts.

"I'm not sure how to answer that," I said with a single tear in my eye. "I guess my life was good. I loved him and I love my family, but, and maybe this is the Patron talking, but I think I lost myself in my marriage."

It was the first time I had ever said it out loud. I had never considered myself as, myself outside of Sam and Corrine.

"Here's the deal, ladies, you all are doing it right." I sat up in my chair. "Keep living **YOUR** life. You are all beautiful, intelligent, and accomplished. Keep focusing on yourself."

"Shiiitttt Gram, if I keep focusing on myself, I'm going to have to buy stock in Duracell!" Livy raised her hands like she was at church,

"Can I get an Amen?" The girls all shouted, "Amen!" Livy was outspoken. I think her career, required her to speak her mind, no matter what. "Listen, Gram. I get what you're saying, but a sista has neeedddsssss, and these batteries are boring the hell out of me. I gots to get me a REAL man, not his bootleg, latex, vibrating cousin!"

The girls burst out in laughter.

"You're just a horny toad, Liv." Nia said.

"Yep. You right!" Liv stood up and model walked toward the bathroom

For the rest of the night we talked about sex and toys, men and work/life balance. I was educated and educating. I learned that being a young Black woman meant that you could map your own course, and that being single didn't mean being alone. I learned that singleness was a badge of honor and that marriage was a choice, rather than a required right of passage like it had been for my generation. More than anything, these women taught me that sex was for women to enjoy too. That was a foreign concept to me. Women could enjoy sex? I had never enjoyed sex with Sam.

When Orlando arrived, several hours after the girls had offed two bottles of Tequila and one bottle of Pinot Grigio, we were knee-deep into Shell's current relationship issues.

She and her boyfriend were on a constant roller coaster of emotions. He was living out-of-state, and she was feeling the pains of wanting him, but fearing that if she had him, she would lose herself. I sat silent as she worked through her dilemma.

"I love him, but I love me more. I can't keep doing the long-distance thing." Shell said through a stream of tears that stained her silk pajamas.

I wish that I had the courage to do that years ago. Orlando offered his perspective as he hugged Shell. "Listen, a man who loves his woman, really loves his woman, will want her to feel whole, complete, and want her to fulfill her dreams. If he is making you choose, then choose...you." I think that was all Orlando said throughout the evening. It was one of many a mic drop moments. *That's what this season meant for me. I was going to choose me.*

We woke up the next morning hungover, in a sea of pizza boxes, and piles of tissues that caught the millions of tears that flowed the night before. I felt new and strange. Traversing the bodies of the Millennials on my way to the kitchen to start a pot of strong coffee, I heard Nia typing away on her laptop. Her voice was groggy, "Hey Gram. Did you have fun last night."

"I had a blast, Nia. Thank you for...well...everything." I wanted to cry, but I didn't. She followed me into the kitchen and leaned against the sink as I was trying to fill the coffee pot. "So, I think I want you to come to the class." She said.

"What cla...that exercise thing that you're doing? Absolutely not!" I had no intention of embarrassing myself in some gym. "No way Nia. I almost broke a hip trying to twerk yesterday."

Nia laughed quietly. "True. But Gram, it'll be good for you. It'll get you outta the house and get your body moving too. Come onnnnnn..." She begged.

"No. Get the coffee out of the pantry." I demanded.

Nia was not the type to take no for an answer. I knew that this was going to be just the beginning of her trying to convince me to participate in her class. I knew it. She knew it. I was determined. She was determined. She was my granddaughter. But I wasn't budging.

Not even for her.

5

Glenn

I recovered from the impromptu slumber party. It took a few days, but I did. Sitting in my backyard, drinking my tea, I recalled that I hadn't seen or heard from Corrine after she stormed out of the house when she found me cleaning out her father's closet. I knew she was hurt. I wanted to make it right with her, so I called her on her cellphone when I knew that she was going to be on the road coming home from the studio. That was the beauty of having a daughter on live television every morning and evening. I could see her. I could hear her. I knew that she was angry and upset. I knew it. She believed that as I packed those bags, that I was throwing away her father and every memory that we had as a family.

"Hello baby."

"Hi Mom." Corrine's tone was cold.

"I haven't talked to you since…how have you been?" I said.

"I've been fine, momma. I'm kinda busy right now. Can we chat later?"

"No, Corrine. I know you're upset. I understand that, but…"

"Do you momma? Do you **REALLY** understand that my dad is dead and you have thrown him and his stuff out. Do you get THAT?"

Corrine was boiling over. I could hear the hurt in her voice. She wasn't angry. She was hurt.

"Listen, baby, I know how it looks. I've been looking at your dad's stuff in the house everyday and I felt like my life was suffocating with his sickness and death. It was just too much." I was weeping. "You have to understand that you and James and Nia get to escape his death, but me… and with his stuff here, in the house, I couldn't escape it, ever."

Corrine wasn't speaking, but I could hear her crying.

"Corrine? Corrine?"

"Yes momma." She said through her brokenness.

"I have some of your dad's things here for you. I want you to come by to get them…tonight. Nia's coming too. We can do dinner at the house. OK?"

"Nia's coming?" Corrine's voice sobered. "I'll be over, but please tell Nia that I am coming so that she can be appropriately dressed when I get there."

Astonishing. Corrine offered additional instructions. No carbs. No red meat. No wine. "We must be done with all of this 'stuff' by 7:00 PM." She demanded. Her daily broadcast started early and she needed her "beauty rest."

"OK Corrine. I'll see you at 6:00 PM. We will eat, cry, and then I'll give you the things that I pulled out for you, OK?"

"Sure, momma. I'll see you then."

I was just about to hang up the phone, when I heard Corrine.

"And momma? I'm sorry. This has been hard and sometimes, I…well…"

"Don't say another word. I understand. I love you and I

understand."

We hung up and I breathed a sigh of relief.

As she worked on her master's degree, Nia was swamped. Her time was constantly occupied with school, thesis research, creating the Seniors Only class, and trying her best to check on me. I, clearly, was a priority, because she visited me daily, even if only for a few moments.

Her adviser, Dr. Philip Turner, required that Nia meet with him every Wednesday at 5:00 PM. She had selected him as her adviser because the rumor around school was that he was very critical of student research. Nia wanted to be challenged, and Professor Turner did just that.

"Come on in, Nia." Professor Turner ushered her into his office.

Nia walked in with her laptop bag and a three-ring binder full of research documents in her hand.

"Hi Professor Turner. How are you?"

"Fine. Nia, have a seat. I want to talk to you about your first draft." Professor Turner had his own three-ring binder opened on his overly crowded desk. Nia sat down.

Professor Turner was a short, Black man with thick, horn-rimmed glasses. His balding head was in need of a clean shave.

"I've been reading through your first draft and I must say, it's very good. Your initial research is well-thought-out and your topic is interesting. I think it's time to put things into practice. How close are you to securing your subjects for the Seniors research?"

Nia wasn't typically nervous, but there was something about Professor Turner that caused tiny beads of sweat to form on her forehead.

"I have to get two more people, a man and a woman. The other 8 couples are ready to go. Oh, and I think that I can convince my grandmother to participate."

"That would be amazing. And the man?"

Nia was scrambling. She was planning to go back to the Senior Center to see if anyone had responded to the sign-up sheet that she placed on the community peg board. She added her flyer to it weeks ago, but hadn't gotten any responses yet.

"I'm going to the center later. I think that I'll have someone." She wasn't sure, but her research, her thesis, and her master's degree depended on finding the last two subjects to study.

"I hope it works out for you. I'd hate for you to have to start all over again."

"Yes. Me too. I will have the participants by close of business next Tuesday. We are set to start classes at Apex Gym on Thursday. I'm on it."

Nia gathered her things and bid Professor Turner goodbye.

Her mind was all over the place as she made her way back to her car. *How in the hell am I going to find 2 more people?*

She picked up her phone as she backed out of the parking space.

"Hello?"

"Hey Grandma!" Nia shouted enthusiastically.

"Uh oh…what do you want child?" I asked suspiciously.

"What makes you think that I want something?" She asked.

"Every time you call me Grandma, I know you want something."

"No…I don't…OK, Gram…I need you to get in this class. Please. I can't finish this thesis without the research and I need 2 more people."

"I told you Nia, I can't. It's not my thing. Call Ruby or Ruth Anne. They may be interested. I'm not in the mood to be around a bunch of strangers, sweatin' and stuff. No. I love you, but no."

"I called them already. Miss Ruby is busy with Cameron and Miss Ruth Anne scares me. Pleeeassseeee Gram?"

Nia was begging at this point.

"Sweetie, I just can't bring myself to do much of anything these days. You understand, right?"

The truth is, I had never told Nia, no. But this time, I just had to. I had no interest in starting anything or meeting people. My new normal was overwhelming enough and I was just getting to the point where I was beginning to feel settled. I certainly didn't want to do anything that would compromise the hard-fought peace that I was gaining in my life.

"I get it Gram. Thanks anyway. I'll see you tomorrow." Nia sounded disappointed, but I think she understood my perspective, even if she didn't like it.

"Oh no. I need you to come over tonight. Your mother is coming and…" Before I could finish, Nia responded.

"No. I can't deal with Corrine tonight. I already feel bad enough. I can't listen to her too. Give her a kiss from me, but I can't deal with her."

"Yeah, like I said, I'll see you at 6:00 PM tonight. I have some things for the two of you from Pop-Pop's closet." I was not taking no for an answer.

"Why is it that you can say no to me, but I can't say no to you?" Nia inquired.

"Because I am your grandmother and what I say goes! See you at 6:00 PM."

We hung up and I nodded my head as though I had won a battle. What was coming, however, was a war.

Having Corrine and Nia in the same space was a calculated risk. I had to operate as Sun Tzu instructed in the *Art of War*. The two would never go to blows, but having them in the same room was as risky as having two opposing countries in a boxing ring. It could, and often did, get nasty.

Right at 6:00 PM, the doorbell rang, and then, I heard the key unlock the door. I wasn't sure which one of them was entering the house. "Hello?"

Corrine shouted back, "It's me momma."

"I'm in the kitchen."

Corrine met me at the dinner table and she embraced me around my neck. "Good to see you, momma. I don't see Nia's car. Is she coming?"

***

Nia stepped out of her car at the park. Every evening, she'd take a run just to clear her head and get a little exercise in. She laced up her shoes, plugged her ears with her AirPods, and started her run. It was 6:05 PM.

'Cause sometimes you just feel tired, feel weak
(Yo left, yo left, yo left, right, left)
And when you feel weak (Yo left)
You feel like you wanna just give up (Yo left, yo left)
But you gotta search within you (Right, left)
Try to find that inner strength (Yo left, yo left)

And just pull that shit out of you (Yo left)
And get that motivation to not give up (Right, left, yo left)
And not be a quitter, no matter how bad you wanna just fall
(Yo left, yo left, right, left)
Flat on your face and collapse

Nate Dogg and Eminem, *Till I Collapse* always made Nia feel strong when she ran. One-half a mile into her run, she saw a dark skinned man on the opposite side of the trail. He was stopped, catching his breath. She could see the flecks of gray in his beard in the distance, and as she got closer, she noticed that he was stretching upward, slowly, to stand up.

The man flagged her down.

"Hi." Nia said.

"Hello." He said.

Nia was out of breath. She removed her AirPods. "Do you need help?"

"Uh. No…well..kind of. I can't seem to connect these things to my phone. I stopped to tie my shoe and now I can't hear anything."

Nia ran over toward him and reached out to grab his AirPods.

"Oh. I see your problem. They need to be charged. Do you have the case?"

"Case? Oh yes, the little box. Yes." He reached into his pocket and pulled out the AirPod case.

Nia put the pods in their respective holes in the charging case. "Uh…so your case is dead too. Sorry. You are going to have to finish your run without music." Nia said as she handed his AirPods and case back.

"Thank you for trying…I'm sorry, I didn't get your name." He said.

"Nia. My name is Nia. And who are you?" She asked.

"Glenn. Glenn Spears." He said.

His Nigerian accent was as smooth as his bald head. He looked fit, but not overly muscular. His body and gray hair said that he was about 70. Nia's wheels began to turn.

"Glenn Spears. Let me ask you a question. I am working on my masters thesis and I am in need of male subjects to study in an exercise class for seniors. Do you mind if I ask you how old you are?"

He chuckled. "I am 75," he said while he flexed like a bodybuilder. "You are a prayer answerer, Nia. I have been looking for a place to workout with a group of folks my age. I am new to Hilbrand and I don't know many people."

"Wow." Nia said. "Well I think that it's your lucky day, Mr. Spears! You would be a welcomed addition to our group. We meet at Apex Gym on Gillam Street on Thursday. There are a total of 8 couples. My research is about the physical activity of male and female seniors. Will you be OK with being partnered up with a woman? I don't want to offend your wife since you and your partner may be in close contact with each other." Nia said.

"Well, I'm not married, and I doubt my ex-wife cares about anything I'm doing. She's busy with her new boyfriend, so…"

Divorced? Perfect. Nia thought.

"Well, that's wonderful. I mean, terrible. I mean…well you know what I mean. And you're in luck! You will be partnered with my grandmother. You both are eager and I think you will hit it off…

working out, I mean. You'll be great workout partners." Nia was red with embarrassment. "We start at 6:00 PM sharp. Dress to sweat. I look forward to seeing you then."

"Wonderful, Nia. I look forward to it. And thanks for the AirPod advice." Glenn turned and waved to Nia as he jogged off.

"Bye Mr. Glenn," she said as she ran the opposite direction. "See you Thursday!" Her mission was calculated. *I'm about to get Gram a man! But I gotta get her to this class first.*

***

Corrine and I waited for Nia for over an hour.

"I knew she wasn't going to come." Corrine said as she began gathering her things. "That girl is on one. I can't understand why she hates me so much."

"Corrine, Nia doesn't hate you. She's busy like you were when you were her age."

"Busy, my ass momma." Corrine said. "She's defiant. I'm tired of her being so entitled. I spent my life doing everything in my power to make sure she had a good life. I'm over her antics. When you see her, tell her that I am disappointed." Corrine was headed to the front door. She had her father's wedding band and the handkerchief in her hand.

"Thank you momma." She said as she clutched the items to her chest.

"Corrine, give her a little grace. It's going to be OK." I said, not sure if I believed myself.

I opened the door, and there stood Nia, primed to put her key in the lock.

"Nice of you to join us…an hour late." Corrine said in a huff. "I'll talk to you later momma." She kissed my cheek, gave Nia a once-over, and sauntered down the walkway toward her car.

"What the hell was that about?" Nia asked with her nose turned up. "I'm just a **little** late."

"Come in Nia." I closed the door behind her, looked up to the sky, and shook my head. *Peace. I just need peace.*

6

I Hear A Symphony

Getting old is overrated. Every morning I wake up to a symphony of cracks and creaks. If it's not my knees, it's my hips. I love the fact that I am still here, but I have to say, the sound of your body breaking down and getting older can be discouraging. I expended so much energy caring and carrying Sam. It felt like my strength died when he did. Sometimes, it takes me a half-hour to get myself out of bed, and two to get my day started. I want nothing more than to reclaim my youth, at least the physical part of it. I had avoided the things in my life that made me feel alive — lunches with my girlfriends, club meetings, and my daily walks. All of that stopped when Sam was diagnosed. I tried to muster up the energy to go out and live normally when Sam was sick, but I never could get it together.

The only other time that I felt that pinch in my being was when we had Corrine. I remember having to plan her outfits, hairstyles, and Asthma medicine the night before any event — holidays, church, or an important outing. I would set out her clothing, bathe her in the best gels, moisturize her delicate skin, comb and tie up her hair, before putting her to bed. When she arose the next morning, I hoped that everything that I had prepared, the night before, was in place. Inevitably, I would find her with her hair bonnet off, her skin ashy, her clothes on the floor, and her bed wet with urine. It was the most frustrating thing. When Sam was sick, I was thrust right back into that world. It would take days for me to prepare Sam's medicine, clothing, care taking, and schedule, just for me to take a walk at the park or get my nails manicured. There was no time to go to lunch with friends, and taking a vacation was out of the question. Caring for a sick spouse is the ultimate test of your vows. The *better* part is easy, the *worse* part is hard. Anyone can live with the health, its that sickness thing that will do you in every time.

All of my relationships suffered. None more so than the one I had with myself. I started to secretly resent my husband and his sickness. I never acted on it, but there were some dark days in those four long years. One thing that I did have were my weekly calls with my sister, Dara. Dara lived in Phoenix with her husband and their only child, a Yorkie named Peanut. She and her husband Floyd had dated for 23 years before they married last year. She and Floyd met decades ago when he was a resident and she was a charge nurse at Turmont Hospital in Garmen, Arizona. There's was a fast, passionate relationship that was taboo at the time. Everyone in our circle wondered why marriage wasn't in the cards for Dara and Floyd, but I knew why they took 23 years to make their way down the aisle. They loved their independence. They have a love affair that most married people could never imagine. I would listen as Dara talked about their escapades and dream about that level of love and passion. Me and Sam, even when he was well, lived very predictable, boring lives. Dinner, TV, sleep was a constant cadence in for our evening. While Dara and Floyd were traveling the world, having unbridled sex all over the globe, I would hope for a glance or a kiss on the cheek when Sam offered his typical, "Good morning, gorgeous" greeting. I couldn't attend the wedding because, well, Sam couldn't travel.

I talked to Dara on Sunday evening, every week, at 6:45 PM. Like clockwork, her call would come just when I needed to hear her voice.

Right on schedule, it was Dara. "Hey sister. It's me." She would say, as though there was anyone else that would call me and address me as sister.

"Hey sister. How are you?" I asked.

"Loving this life and living in bliss. How are you?"

"I'm fine." I wasn't.

Sensing my lie, Dara asked, "What is going on sister? You don't sound like yourself."

"Oh…Dara…It's hard. It's so hard." I lamented for 20 minutes. I poured out my heart to her and wept. She listened and didn't say a word. Her silence allowed me to finally hear my grief, my anger, my denial, my sadness, and my negotiation that I had done with God. After a while, I, in my grief, grew silent. Dara breathed in, then exhaled hard.

"Sister? I have heard you. I listened and I heard you." She inhaled and exhaled hard again. "Do you want me to tell you the truth, or do you want me to lie to you?" I knew Dara and I knew that no matter what I said, she was going to give me the truth, straight, no chaser. I breathed deeply.

"Truth."

"Sister, the way I see it is that you have one foot in the grave and one out. You have to shift your weight and make a decision. You need to either get busy living, or get busy dying. It's that simple."

Tears welled up behind my closed eyelids.

She continued, "Sam is dead and he's not coming back…ever. You are a vibrant, beautiful woman with a tremendous amount of life to still live and you don't have time to waste. Whatever you put your energy to is what will grow in your life. Watering your grief, grows your grief. Watering your life, grows your life. Pick, sister."

I hated that she was right. I was dying inside. My life was a continuing saga of sadness and doing what the world expected me to do. I wept more because I didn't want to die, I just didn't know how to live. Dara's words cut like a hot knife through butter. They were harsh and honest, and exactly what I needed. "Sister, oh my dear sister, I love you." I said.

"I love you. Shift your weight, sister and live." Dara said.

"Until next week." I said.

"Until next week." Dara replied.

We hung up, and I started to shift.

7

One...Just One

"But Grammmmmm...you have to come! I need more participants and you are exactly the demographic that I need for my research."

Nia was begging at this point. For the past 3 days, she called and begged. She came over and begged. She even sent me a text, begging me to participate. Now, she was at the house, begging me again. This would be her last-ditch effort to try to get me to her Seniors Only exercise class.

"Listen, sweetheart, I'd love to help you, but I'm old and I have no desire to get into some old persons exercise class. How many times do I have to say it? No!" I shook my head and shooed her away, "No. Nope. I'm not going."

"But Gram, I need you. I have one more slot to fill and I need a female subject." Nia was sitting on the floor at my feet, holding onto my shins, and whining at this point. I was reading, "Seat of the Soul" by Eckart Tolle, seeking peace, when I peeked over the pages to see her smooth brown skin and her desperate eyes.

"Dear Lord, Nia! You are relentless. OK. One class. That's it Nia! Just one." I closed the book on my lap as she leaped from the floor to give me a bear hug.

"Thank you, Gram! You won't regret it. I promise." Nia bounded out of the house, and I sat in Sam's chair wondering what I had just agreed to. It didn't matter. My granddaughter was happy and I, apparently, was about to embark upon a fitness journey, at 73 years-old. *What the hell was I thinking?*

The following Thursday, I walked into the gym dressed in a pair of baggy sweatpants that I dug out of my closet, and a tee-shirt that read *Best Grandma Ever*. Nia had given it to me on the birthday before Sam's diagnosis. It was the last happy birthday that I spent with him. A sea of old people greeted me at the door. *Lordy bee... I'm one of them.* Nia popped over and introduced me to the other members of the class. It was like a family reunion where no one knew each other. We hugged and hi-fived like we were all old friends.

"So Gram, everyone has a workout partner and we make the matches co-ed. One man, one woman. My thesis is all about the differences in physical ability of men and women as they age." I nodded like I understood what she was saying. "You will stay with your partner for the duration of the project." I shot Nia a look.

"Sweetheart, I said one day. I never agreed to an indefinite time working out."

I spoke softly enough so she would be the only one that heard me, and I didn't move my mouth. My mother called it *van-mom-a-quism*. Every mother knows how to do it. We can carry on a full conversation, smiling, without moving our mouths at all like a ventriloquist. I had perfected the art. Nia smiled wide and mouthed, *"I know."* I watched as she paired up each couple. Thelma with Harry, Gloria with Andy, Marshall with Yvonne. Nine couples in all. I waited my turn to be paired up, but quickly noticed that there wasn't a male partner for me. Eureka! No partner, no class! I sighed a breath of relief and reached for my gym bag when the glass door flung open. There, walking through the door, was a dark-skinned gentleman with the brightest smile I had ever seen. He was dressed in long red gym shorts and a clingy white shirt that bore the Nike swoosh on the left side of his chest.

"Mr. Glenn, you made it! I am so glad you came. We were just about to start." He dropped his bag in the pile with the others, and Nia guided him my way.

"Gram, this is Glenn Spears, your partner," Nia said with a hint of glee in her voice. Glenn was tall and he had to look down slightly to catch my eye.

"Good evening. Your name?" His voice was strong and he had a distinct Nigerian accent. I stood still as my mouth grew dry. *What was my name?*

"Doris. My name is Doris Ashworth, but you can call me Doris."

What the hell was I saying? I was acting like a star struck teenager. This man, in a matter of moments, took my breath, and my ability to speak away. He was handsome, charming, and he smelled delightful. Nia's voice knocked me back into reality.

"OK everybody, we are going to start with some light stretches. Everyone on the floor. If you have trouble getting down, ask your partner to help you." She said.

Glenn and I walked to the blue and red mats that were perfectly positioned on the floor. I could feel the other women in the class boring holes in the back of my head. Although this wasn't a class designed to ogle folks, Glenn sure was easy on the eye and the pick of the litter in this sea of seniors. Hell, Glenn would be the pick no matter the litter.

"Shall we sit?," he asked.

I slid my frame on the mat when Nia instructed, "OK kids, legs open, toes touching, and if you can, grab each other's hands."

Glenn met me on the floor, and we spread our legs. *What the hell?* I had been flexible in my youth, but age had caught up to me and my muscles. Glenn was able to stretch his legs pretty wide, but he shortened his expanse to meet mine.

"Don't spread them too far. I don't want you to hurt yourself." He said slyly.

Was he flirting or was he really concerned about the condition of my inner thighs?

"I won't. Thank you." I said as he took my hands in his. We pushed and pulled each other for a few minutes until Nia instructed us to move.

"Time to change position, Doris." *Change position? I like where we are now. Good Lord! Everything this man says seems sexual...and I liked it.*

The one-hour class seemed like it lasted an eternity. Glenn was a wonderful partner. We stretched, lifted light weights, and meditated before class was over.

"Alright kids, I'll see you on Wednesday. Don't forget to hydrate," Nia said. I reached for my gym bag to retrieve a towel to dab the sweat that had gathered on my forehead.

"I haven't sweat this much in ages." I joked as Glenn walked past.

"Pity. You should really sweat more often. It's good for the body and the soul." He winked.

Before I could react to his comment, he was gone through the glass doors that led to the parking lot. I stood there, sweating.

After the rest of the class had left, Nia slid up to me with a grin so wide, she looked like a cat who had just caught a canary.

"Welllllll….what do you think about the class Gram?" Her arms were crossed in front of her chest, and she was shifting her weight from side-to-side like a pendulum.

"It was very nice. Informative and nice." I said modestly.

"Nice my ass Gram!!!! That man is FIIIINNNNNEEEEE!!!! Why do you think I partnered the two of you up together! He's Zaddy for real!"

I didn't know what a Zaddy was, but Nia and I giggled talking about Glenn.

"You know he looks good!" Now I was sweating **AND** blushing. I couldn't seem to cool down. Nia continued, "Gram. It's OK to have a little flirty fun."

He *was* handsome and he had a way about him. Dare I say, sexy. I suppose Nia could see the glint in my eye. I hadn't flirted with anyone since, well, never. Sam wasn't the "flirty" type. His ex-military ways were straight and to the point. When he asked me to marry him, he knelt on one knee and said, "We should get married and have children. It's time." Not exactly moonlight and roses, but he made his point and it worked because I said "Yes." This man, Glenn was different. He certainly was handsome, but I had no interest in getting to know him on any level, least of which romantically. I had loved and lost and at 73, my love life was over. It, and my desire for romance died the day that we buried Sam. Who was I kidding! This feeling, the giddy, sexy feeling that I had thinking about Glenn awakened a part of me that I didn't recognize. I wanted to feel it more and secretly, I wanted to feel him.

Slow down Doris. Don't get ahead of yourself.

My declaration of a one-time workout turned into 3 days a week of sweating and lusting after Glenn. Nia was crafty. She baited me to the gym with promises of fitness, and I stayed because of promises of something else. I had been working out with Glenn and we even had a few post-workout juice bar dates. I can't say that we were dating, we were just drinking juice and working out together, all while I would listen to his deep voice and stare into his piercing dark brown eyes. Dating was for young people. We weren't dating because we weren't young.

I had managed to wake up early in the morning, just in time to see the sun rise. I rolled out of my bed and pressed my feet to the floor. That sensation of planting my feet on solid ground always made me feel alive. Probably because when Sam was alive, I never savored the little things. I was moving so fast in those days that there were times that I couldn't remember if I had eaten. It wasn't about me. It was never about me. I breathed in deeply and closed my eyes. My morning meditation is where I center myself. It allows me to connect with God and my soul. It is a welcomed addition to my daily routine. My life, now, was full and whole. More so now than ever before. It had been about a year since I lost Sam and although I missed him, I was settling into my new normal.

Corrine was still grieving deeply over the death of her father, and Nia was now in her last year of graduate school. Having Glenn in my life was thrilling. Our non-date, dates, were something for me to look forward to every week. I had even reconnected with my friends. For the 4 years before Sam's death, I had cut myself off from almost everyone. I stopped going to the Highlands meetings, the Sunday calls with Dara had become shorter and less frequent, and I wasn't able to go to my weekly lunches with my two best friends. They all indulged me while Sam was sick, but recently, my friends were demanding more girl time.

Ruby and Ruth Ann understood my struggles while I was caring for Sam, but now, that a bit of time had passed since his death, they wanted to have lunch. I was jolted out of my meditation with the sound of *My Girl* blasting from my phone. Nia had taught me how to program a ring tone to a specific person. Ruth Ann was a huge Temptations fan, and she was *my girl*. Her ring tone was apropos.

"Hello Ruthy girl." I was happy to see her name on the screen and hear her voice in my ear.

"Listen Dor, me and Ruby are sick of you telling us that you can't make our lunch date! I'm coming over at noon. Be ready! We miss you and have so much to talk about." I knew that Ruth Ann was serious. She was a retired accountant who once owned her own practice, then ceremoniously sold it to the highest bidder three years later. She was rich, RICH! She drove a custom Range Rover on the weekdays, and a Phantom on the weekends. She sold the family home and bought a penthouse in the city so that she could have 24-hour concierge service and a restaurant to dine at that was on the street level of her building when she didn't feel like cooking. Her son, Cameron, went to school that is two doors from her building, so she was able to walk him there every day. She was living her best life.

She continued talking about how she missed me and how I was

never around and needed to get out of the house. I listened to her symphony of complaints. Determined as ever, Ruth Ann was not the type to take no for an answer. Even if I wanted to object, I couldn't. She would not have it. She and her husband divorced decades ago, and they masterfully co-parented their children -- all 5 of them. Her eldest son, Cameron lived with her. Her other children were peppered across the country making their mark in their chosen professions -- a doctor, two lawyers, and a beekeeper. Yes, a beekeeper. Cameron is Autistic, and though he is non-verbal, Ruth Ann had a special way of communicating with him, and he with her. It's called tapping. Each tap means something different --*yes, no, wait, macaroni* and *cheese, bathroom*. It was like they created another language all their own.

"So be ready! Ruby is going to meet us at Denim. We aren't taking 'no' for an answer." I had avoided them for as long as I could. They were my dearest friends and I needed to open them up to my new life. They counseled and comforted me through my old one, now, it was time to share my new one.

I looked at my watch, *11:56 AM*. As I made the final touches to my hair, the doorbell rang.

"Comingggggg...." I yelled.

"Open the door, diva!" Ruth Ann yelled back. I took a last glance at myself in the hallway mirror, grabbed the brass door handle, and pulled it open.

"Divvvaaaaa!!!!" We squealed at each other, arms outstretched.

"You look amazing Dor!!!" I placed my index finger on top of my head and twirled like a ballerina in a music box. Ruth Ann had always been petite. She didn't work out, nor did she eat right, but her body was always fit and fabulous.

"What in the hell have you been doing? You look amazing." I hadn't noticed any real changes in my body since I started working out with Nia and Glenn. I felt different, but I hadn't considered that I looked different.

"I'm doing this exercise class with Nia, but we can talk about that over lunch. Let's go before Ruby starts cussing people out." What I really wanted to say was, *I kept my vows and cared for Sam. I loved him, and now, I am learning to love me. Oh...and there's another man that sends shock waves through my body when I see him.* But, I didn't.

Ruby was a quick trigger. Any and everything could set her off. One time, we were at the movies and the previews took longer than she thought they should. This woman proceeded to cuss out the manager of the theater and threatened to contact the production company and the corporate office to complain. She caused such a scene, that she was banned from the theater for life! Ruth Ann and I still laugh at the fact that Ruby's picture is hanging in the box office. She was a stickler for time and often told us, "Early is on time. On time is late. And late is unacceptable." If we were a minute past noon, we, and everyone else in the restaurant would have to hear about it.

"Yeah, let's go before Ruby goes rogue." We laughed hysterically.

As we rounded the corner after parking Ruth Ann's car, we could already hear Ruby going off on someone.

"Oh Lord." Ruth Ann said. "What is she fussin' about now?"

Ruby was a heavy-set woman with pale skin and a flaming red mane of hair that reflected her fiery personality. She had been a CFO of a major corporation and had worked her way to the top. She said, on many occasions, "I didn't get to where I am by being nice." She wasn't a mean person, just focused, direct, and a ball-buster. If you wanted anything done, you called Ruby.

As we approached the entrance of the restaurant, we heard her, "How hard is it to add ice to water? I'm not asking for the moon here. Just some damn ice." She turned and saw me and Ruth Ann.

Without missing a beat, she said, "Hey divas." She quickly turned back to the hostess that was standing at the door.

"Get me your manager!" Ruth Ann and I stepped into the doorway.

"Umm…ma'am?" We were addressing the server as she looked too afraid to speak. "Everything is fine. May we be seated?"

The young server looked like she had seen a ghost. She was terrified.

I grabbed Ruby by the hand and whispered, "You gon' be banned from here like the theater and you KNOW you like this bread. We will get you your damn ice. Just smile and come on!"

Ruby faked a smile and walked slowly toward the table. We sat down and I immediately started laughing.

"You always startin' something! I've missed you and your craziness, Ruby."

Denim was the perfect setting for this girl's day out. It was a trendy restaurant that opened a few years back. Owned by Derrick and French Deneem, a bi-racial, openly gay couple, Denim was Hilbrand's first comfort food restaurant. Here, you could munch on everything from meatloaf made with beef, pork, and lamb to grilled cheese sandwiches made with homemade bread and a variety of imported cheeses. The décor looked like you stepped into a *Millers*

Outpost. Hues of blue were everywhere, from the walls to the seating. Denim was a celebration of all-American food and all-American design. The seats were fashioned out of old jeans and the white linen napkins were folded like pockets with the silverware tucked neatly inside.

"Child…that lil' girl was about to get it!" Ruby said with her Southern drawl hanging in the air like limbs of a willow tree. "She don't know who she's dealin' with! I'm Rubystein Harris!" She snapped her fingers, and we all broke out in laughter. We spent the better part of the afternoon talking about our children and grandchildren, trading pictures and stories, and had a tender moment when we talked about how we had all met.

All of our children were around the same age and had gone to school together from elementary all the way to their junior year in high school. The kids had known each other their entire lives. Corrine, and Ruby's son Ernest, were great friends, and they were leaders in school. Cameron was often bullied, and Corrine and Ernest started a club that supported kids that were bullied. The Anti-Bullying Club was designed to encourage students to stop bullying and celebrate the differences of each student. The A.B.C. was a model club on the campus of Hilbrand High, and Corrine and Earnest were recognized by the city council for their efforts. On the night of the awards ceremony, Ruby went home and found Earnest hanging from his bedroom closet. He left a note that said that he had been living a lie and didn't deserve to live anymore. He didn't offer any other information. We never learned what troubled him so deeply that he would take his own life, but after that day, Ruby was understandably never the same. Our families bonded over our collective sorrow when Earnest died and our friendship, as mothers, deepened. From that point forward, we have been inseparable, until Sam's diagnosis and subsequent death turned me into a hermit. I hid from them for years and now, like a butterfly, I was emerging from my cocoon, ready to fly.

"So what's been going on with you Miss Doris? You lookin' real cute." Ruby spoke in a way that let me know that she knew something about me or maybe even Glenn.

"Whatever do you mean?" I replied mimicking her Southern drawl.

"Well if you're going to act coy, then I'm gonna just say what I know." Ruth Ann sat up in her chair.

"What's going on? What are you hiding?"

Ruby started in, "Well, Doris over here has been cavorting with a man! Not just any man, a finnnnneeeee man." My cheeks were flush and I almost spit out the sip of Pinot Grigio that was in my mouth.

"What? How? What are you talking about?" My words were clumsy like a toddler learning to walk.

"A man?" Ruth Ann screamed. Heads of the other diners turned our direction. I bowed mine in embarrassment.

"Oh yes child, a man!" Ruby continued, "My girlfriend Thelma is in the exercise class with our fair Doris and her boyfriend. From what I hear, they are a thing and furthermore, the other ladies in the class are none too happy about it. Apparently, this man is the talk of the town and is VERY easy on the eye."

"Good lord Ruby. Stop. I am not some horny teenager." I tried to compose myself. My speech was proper and curt. "Glenn is **JUST** a friend, and we work out together because Nia paired us up. That's all."

I tried my best to not to show my glee in just saying his name. I was like a youngster. The mere mention of his name made me smile inside.

"Well, all I'm going to say is that you deserve happiness. I know it was hard when Sam got sick. You have been everybody's everything for ages. It's your time in the sun." Ruth Ann raised her glass for a toast. Ruby followed suit.

"Here's to basking in the glow of the sun. Let us not burn under its rays, but rather find shelter in the shadow of love and friendship." I raised my glass.

"To shelter in the sun." I said.

"To shelter in the sun." Ruby replied. As we took a sip of our drinks, I closed my eyes and grinned to myself. I longed for Glenn to become my shelter.

8

Banana Split

"Five, 4, 3, 2, 1..." Nia's voice was loud and echoed throughout the gym as we finished the last exercise of our dreaded leg day.

"I hate lunges." I said it loud enough for Nia to hear me. She cut me a look, and then smiled at me. Glenn was stretching on the floor and he burst into laughter.

"It appears as though our trainer is displeased with your commentary," he said. I cut him a look too.

I knelt down to reach the floor to begin our cool down stretching routine. Glenn raised his hand to help me down. I smacked it away.

"I got it." I said as I struggled to get to the floor. My thighs were throbbing and I was dreading the day that I said 'yes' to Nia about joining this class. "I swear, this child is trying to kill us." My bottom hit the floor and Glenn reached for my hands again.

"Come. Stretch Doris. When we are done, I'll treat you to a smoothie." He said as we pushed and pulled together to loosen our muscles. I smiled sweetly as I looked at Glenn.

"I deserve it."

"Yes, you do," he agreed.

We finished our stretching and were inching our way to the door. Nia stopped us in our tracks.

"I heard what you said, Gram." She was standing with her hands on her hips as though she was scolding me.

"I know!" I said with just as much attitude.

Glenn stood back and watched our pseudo-grudge match. "Can we put a pin in this conversation. I'd like to take this lovely lady for a smoothie."

Nia stopped mid-sentence. "Oh…so is this a date, date?" She was grinning hard.

"No." Glenn and I said at the same time.

"Yeah, right. OK, y'all have fun then. I mean, I could use a smoothie, but you know…I didn't get an invitation, so…" Nia's sarcasm was hilarious.

"No, you're not invited! If you cut out those lunges next time, I might let you have a sip of my smoothie." I said as I pushed passed her and interlocked arms with Glenn.

He waved goodbye, and Nia was left standing with a huge grin on her face. We walked, arm-in-arm the few blocks to the Banana Split.

"Your granddaughter is crafty." Glenn said as we scanned the menu that was overhead.

"What can I get you?" The cashier asked. She was a young, blonde girl with piercing blue eyes. She was overly bubbly and friendly, like she had taken several straight shots of wheatgrass.

"I'll have a large strawberry banana with a shot of whey protein and ginger."

"And for your wife?" She said.

Glenn looked at me and he motioned for me to order.

"We aren't married. But I will have a large blueberry and mango."

"Oh…OK…I'm sorry. I just thought…" The cashier was apprehensive and nervous.

"It's fine. We are lovers." Glenn said, his Nigerian accent floated through the room like a fragrance.

My eyes got wide and I blushed. *Lovers?* "Ummm…no we aren't…we are…Lord Glenn." I sat down at a table, completely embarrassed and secretly hopeful that one day his joke would become reality.

Glenn came to the table with two enormous cups in his hands.

"Lord! I said large, not gigantic! Thank you."

He reached over to me and we toasted our cups.

"So, Doris Ashworth, I am glad that you agreed to come with me today. I have had your sweat dripping on me, held your waist while supporting you doing your first push up, and spread your legs far and wide. But I don't know you. Who are you Doris Ashworth?"

I looked up at him after taking a long swig of my smoothie. It was sweet and cold on my tongue.

"What do you want to know, Glenn Spears?"

"Everything."

I blushed and took another swig. I took a deep breath and started telling him about me, Corrine, Nia, James, and Sam. I talked to him about my best friends and my sister Dara. He sat attentive, asking questions ever so often.

"You and Nia are very close, yes?" He inquired.

"Very. Nia is an amazing young woman. She is funny, witty, and fiercely passionate about everything that she loves."

"She is also crafty." Glenn sat back in his chair. "She is calculated, for sure."

"What do you mean?" I asked.

"I met Nia a few days before starting with the class. She told me that I was going to partner with her grandmother, but you hadn't agreed to join the class at that time. She has been playing matchmaker with us."

I thought back on her insistence about me joining. She was lackadaisical at first, but after that night that she came over late, her persistence became a daily, annoying occurrence. Glenn and I figured that when she met him, she had put her plan in motion.

"Oh my God! I'm gonna kill that child." I was horrified. "I was set up! We were set up?"

Glenn was grinning ear-to-ear. "You say that like it's a bad thing, Doris." He reached for my hand and touched it gently. "Is it a bad thing, Doris?"

I squirmed in my seat. "No, I suppose it isn't." A crash of thunder broke the tension. "Rain, really?"

The downpour peppered the window of the Banana Split and we watched as the wetness changed the color of the asphalt, and pedestrians ran for cover. I hate driving in the rain. "Ummm…can we go? I hate driving in the rain and I want to get home before it really starts coming down."

"Absolutely." Glenn said as he stood and walked to pull out my chair. I gathered my smoothie and my gym bag.

Glenn followed behind me and opened the glass door of the Banana Split.

We walked swiftly down the street toward my car. Reaching the intersection of Gillam and Fort, the street was flooding. All I could think about was how to cross without soaking my feet and ruining my new shoes. I stopped short, and Glenn could sense my dilemma. Before I could assess my strategy to get across the street, Glenn scooped me up in his arms and carried me to the next corner. He gently placed my feet on the pavement and grabbed my hand as we continued walking to my car. I was speechless. No one had ever carried me, anywhere. Sam didn't even carry me across the threshold when we returned from our honeymoon.

We reached my car. "Shall I follow you home?" Glenn asked. He was wet and his shirt was sticking to his chest and I could see his muscles. The rain drops streamed down his face like a river.

"Uh…n..no. I think that I can take it from here. Thank you." He reached for my bag, opened my rear door and placed the bag on the seat. He was getting soaked.

"I will see you next class, Doris Ashworth." Glenn reached his head into the car and he kissed me. Passionately. I was shocked and satisfied. He reached for my cheek with his hand and I pulled away from him. Until that moment, I hadn't kissed another man in 50 years.

"Uh…Yes. Next class." I said. "Thank you." *Thank you? What was I thanking him for? Geez. I have no idea what I'm doing!* I closed my car door and drove off. I checked my rear view mirror and watched as Glenn and his wet body jogged through the parking lot to his car. I whispered to myself, *"Damn."*

9

Finding…Me

By now, Glenn and I had gone out a few times and my feelings for him were growing like weeds. Untamed and wild, I sometimes let my thoughts about him run free. I'd find myself daydreaming about his smile and how it lit up the room when he walked into the gym. I stood mesmerized as he stretched before our workouts. He would glance my way before approaching me. He seemed to barely touch the ground when he walked, and he would have the most suggestive greetings. One day, he came in the room in a black-on-black Nike dri-fit shirt and lose fitting workout pants. He dropped his bag and stood on the side of me, close enough for me to feel the heat of his body on mine.

He opened his mouth and said, "Are you ready to get wet?" I blushed and was rendered speechless. After a few seconds, I managed to clutch my chest and ask, "What?" Slyly, he pulled away from me and said, "I heard we were doing aqua aerobics today." He walked away after a wink and a smile. I was left with all sorts of unholy thoughts running through my head. Glenn has a way. He's sexy and sensual, but not vulgar.

After the series of exchanges, I was beginning to look forward to his saunters through the door of the gym and his suggestive quips as he greeted me. We hadn't gone to bed with one another, but Lord knows I wanted to. I had never really felt this level of passion or attraction to a man before. Sam was my first and only. Well, at least that's the story I told him before we married. He died believing that he was. I don't apologize for my lie. In my day, ladies didn't discuss their sexual exploits, and virginity was a powerful and necessary requirement to seal your status as a "good girl." Chastity was revered and celebrated. In fact, the idea of having multiple sexual partners was taboo and reserved only for the girls with no morals. Yes, in my day, saving yourself for marriage was the only way to be for young women. Interestingly, that same sentiment didn't hold true for men. Men and boys were encouraged to "sow their wild oats" before marrying the "old ball-and-chain," ever depriving them of having any other woman in their beds. I never asked Sam how many partners he had, but I can imagine with his military service and the cultural acceptability of male sexual freedom, there were several before me. It was assumed by all, I suppose, that I was a virgin on our wedding night. The truth is that I had a torrid love affair during a summer in Rome when I was a sophomore in college.

Rome, 1968

I had been selected to participate in a student exchange program and at the time, it was highly unusual for a Black woman to travel abroad to study in a foreign country. I was eager to get on the plane and experience different food and culture. When I stepped foot in Italy, I felt at home. There was something about the air and the ease of the people that drew me in. I caught a taxi to my sponsor's apartment in Trieste. I was met by a beautiful Italian woman named Alma Di Grazia.

She was a world renowned philosophy professor at the prestigious University of Rome, and under her tutelage, I would be studying the great philosophers: Plato, Socrates, Aquinas, and Xenophanes. She was magnificent. Dark olive skin with long mahogany-toned hair. Her Romanesque features were prominent, none more than her almond-shaped, deep brown eyes that could pierce the darkness of night. She was effervescent and free in her movements. During this tumultuous season, she stressed the importance of women becoming empowered in every area of their lives, including sexually. I had arrived in 1968. While the United States was in an uproar and at the height the Civil Rights Movement, Rome was experiencing student-led protests at almost every university. Italy had just formed its own economy and was becoming more and more industrialized, and the Cold War was seeing triumphs in socialism and political upheaval. Students, who drove the movement, challenged the new capitalist society that disproportionately harmed regular workers. I was in Rome on March 1, 1968 when the Battle of Valle Giulia commenced at Rome University. I watched as youth were demonstrating in the same ways that Blacks were demonstrating halfway around the world. I was inspired and thought that I would never leave Italy.

One day, as I sat on a grassy knoll on campus, I was approached by a man. He told me that his name was Givano. He asked, "May I sit?" I obliged and we began talking about the plight of young Italians and Black people and how, we, as the youth of the day, could change the world. He was tall, thin, and looked more African than Italian. His olive skin glowed and his blue eyes looked like ice cubes. I wasn't sure what he was. African, American, or Aboriginal. He was non-descriptive and exotic. He spoke with an accent that I hadn't heard before. I asked where he was from and he said, "Madagascar."

Before I could inquire further, he asked if I wanted to go to a local café for dinner. Four hours of chatting over piles of gnocchi, turned into 3 hours of lovemaking in my room at Alma's.

We entered my room, hand-in-hand. There was no conversation, but more than enough communication. My bed rested on the floor, in the far left corner, underneath a window that faced a cobblestone alley. The sway of drying laundry on the clotheslines, from the neighboring building, were swaying in the wind like wings of a bird. He and I stood face-to-face, basking in our collective energy. His olive complected hand reached for my shoulder, and in one swift motion, he released my flowing white, cotton blouse from my right, then my left side. It slid down to my waist exposing my supple breasts. He reached his hand gently to touch me, and instead of caressing my swelling mounds, he placed his bare hand between them. I could feel my heart racing, but I was calm. Before I could think, I reached my hands over his and began unbuttoning his green short-sleeved shirt. Under it rested a chiseled chest. He was thin, but extremely muscular and his chest looked like olive mountains, one rippling higher that the next. He took my hand in his and dragged it across his bare body, directing me to his pants. I could feel him hardening, and I sensed his size and girth. I struggled to release him from the confines of his khaki's. Seeing my difficulty, he reached down to assist me. First, the button, then the zipper. His now, granite hard penis was protruding long enough to touch my thigh. I was in awe of its size. I couldn't imagine my body being large enough to accept his. He turned me around so that my back was to him, and he lifted my skirt. My knees began to weaken and I knelt on the bed, kicking my skirt all the way off on my way down. My curiosity caused me to turn and lay on my back with my legs in a butterfly position. I closed my eyes, tight.

*I can't tell you why, but I felt a deep attraction to him. He was skilled and gentle. I felt empowered because I had chosen to lay with him. Our lovemaking lasted, for what seemed to be hours. Our bodies stayed in sync and the rush of pleasure was almost unbearable. As we crescendoed, I felt the orgasm so deeply, I cried. It wasn't that I didn't like it, on the contrary, I liked it **TOO** much. This wasn't anything like my mother had described sex to be. She was less than informative, but what she did say was, "Sex is awful and should only be done if you are trying to have children. Let your husband do his business and then make him a meal." Never in my life had I had the desire to be so reckless, but it felt so right. I don't remember Givano's last name, I just know that one night, after too much pasta and red wine, my life changed. It was raw and beautiful, and I swore that night that I would never have sex again until I was married. I made a conscious decision to restrain my sexual urges until then, so that I could unleash them on my husband.*

***

Sam and I had been together on a regular basis during our marriage, but it never reached the level of passion that I experienced in Rome. Our lovemaking was regimented and boring. Perhaps it was because Sam was ex-military and very reserved in his everyday life, or maybe it was because sex was always on purpose, and it was never unfettered and spontaneous. There was always a reason to be intimate: birthday, holiday, promotion at work, trying to conceive a baby. It was based on utility and not pleasure. I imagined that being with Glenn would be different. He hadn't touched me at all, yet I felt a different kind of attraction and stirring when he was just near me. Ours, if it were to ever happen, would be for sheer pleasure for me for the first time in my life. It wasn't quite the Romanesque type of attraction, but it was a more mature version of what I felt those decades before in that apartment in Trieste.

That Sunday, like clockwork, my phone rang.

"Hey sister. It's me." Dara's voice was a welcomed part of my day.

"Hey sister. I'm doing great!" I said with enthusiasm.

"OK, Miss Girl, what has gotten into you?"

He hasn't been in me…yet, I thought.

"Nothing." I said coyly. "But I met a man."

"Awwww shit now. I told you to shift, and shift you did! Details, child. Details." Dara demanded.

I told her all about Glenn. The Nigerian accent, the body, the eyes, the flirty way we communicated, and his "way."

"Sister…he has a *way* about him. The kids call it swagger." I giggled. "When he walks it's like he glides. And girl, he smells like… oooo, I can't even describe it. He smells like he would taste like warm sweet cake."

"Alright now, Doris. I ain't mad at you." Dara laughed hysterically.

Dara and I kee-keed for an hour. I was turning into Nia and Livy and Shell. I need my own tribe of "besties" to spill tea and dish with.

We hung up and I laughed to myself.

10

Size Matters

After those first few weeks of working out, Nia encouraged me to try wearing jeans one more time. She said, "Gram, all those squats we have been doing in class are paying off! We need that booty in some jeans!" We went to the Francis, a trendy shop in the Hilbrand Mall. Walking in, I thought I was going to have a stroke. The music was deafeningly loud and there were salespeople on skates sailing through the store's round displays helping customer after customer. Nia spotted a salesperson that she knew by name.

"Malin!" She yelled. Just then, a tall Nordic looking White boy turned toward us and skated our way.

"DIVAAAAAAA Niaaaaaaa!" He squealed. The two engaged one another with a series of "yassss girrlllls" and "werk queens" as they spun, snapped, and twirled together. Seconds later, Malin turned to me, staring deep into my eyes and then glancing over my form, "Nia...who is your fierce friend?" I did a judgmental once-over on Malin and said, "I am Nia's GRANDMOTHER!" Malin seemed to feign a stumble from his skates and said, "Well grandmother, you are finnnneeeeee!" I giggled at his obvious overreaching compliment. I have never been self-conscious, but I'm not a Millennial, and I am aware that I don't turn heads or see myself as worthy of compliments in that manner. Malin turned his attention back to Nia, "What are we looking for today Diva!" Nia stepped closer to me and placed her arm around my shoulder, "My grandmother has a man, and she needs some jeans." I was horrified. I cut my eyes at Nia and said through clenched teeth, "He is just a friend." Malin grabbed my hand and whispered, "Aren't they all?"

We floated behind Malin as we entered the denim section of the Francis. The store was unisex and sizes were not visible on any of the clothing tags. I learned later that the store owner was a transgender woman that decided that labels and tags were too limiting, even in clothing. I thought it was an interesting concept, expect for the fact that there would be no way of knowing which pants would fit me. Malin then ushered me to the mirror. It was unassuming and full length with the words, "You Are Perfect" inscribed at the very top center of its heavily gilded frame. There had to be hundreds of them all over the store, a different saying on each one.

"Now, Grand Diva, this is how we size at the Francis. These mirrors are interactive and there is a little camera inside of it that tells us which rack to go to for your perfect jeans." I didn't understand what he was saying, but I stood in front of the mirror with my hands clenched at my sides.

"Ummm Gram, unless you want to add more size to your hips, you're going to have to raise your arms all the way up over your head." I looked at Nia and she demonstrated. I handed her my black Chanel purse and stood straight in front of the mirror. I raised my arms over my head as though I was attempting to dive into the clear reflective pool of glass before me. The mirror had a small red light in the upper left corner that flashed.

"OK Gram, don't move." Malin instructed. In a flash, a blue solid light shone, and the mirror began to flicker with a soft white light. Moments later, a number appeared. *I-899*. Malin squealed, "OK miss girl, let's go this way. Nia, keep Gram's bag, we have shopping to do!" Malin and I got to rack I-899 and a sea of denim jeans awaited our selection. Who knew there were so many shades of blue! I settled on three pairs of, what Malin called, "Mom jeans re-imagined." They were high in the waist and were made with four-way stretch cotton.

"They are made with a forgiving fabric, Gram. These jeans will hug, not hurt, every curve. You have worked so hard at the gym and now it's time to show off your hard work." Nia said.

After checking out and getting back to the car, I was exhausted and excited.

"Nia, thank you sweetheart. I am learning a whole new world with you, and I appreciate everything that you have done for me since Pop Pop…well…you know."

"Oh Gram, you're the best. I love you!" After a quick hug and kiss on the cheek, Nia dropped me back off at my house and I flopped onto the easy chair. For the first time in a long time, I came home and the first thing on my mind wasn't about being in the house alone. I felt free and happy. I didn't wonder if Sam was going to be on the other side of the door. Everything was exactly as I had left it. Part of me felt regret that I was feeling so light, and the other part felt the joy inching back into my life.

11

Check Please

The following week, I had my best workout yet. Nia had us doing all cardio and I had run faster and farther than ever before. Glenn and I were the stars of our class and we had become quite fit. I was feeling so good that, after class, I decided to sit in the steam room to reward myself for all my hard work. When I was done and dressed, I went back into the main gym looking for Glenn. He was gone. I figured that he was going to wait for me, but he hadn't. As I was fumbling in my gym bag searching for my keys, I got a phone call. It was Glenn.

"Hello?"

"Hello Doris. It's me."

"Hi, I missed seeing you after class today. Are you OK?" I asked.

"Fine. Just had to take care of some business at the house. The plumber came to snake the drains. Hey, I was wondering, are you free for lunch tomorrow?" I smiled inside because he was asking me on a REAL date. It felt like high school all over again.

"Ummm…unfortunately, I'm unavailable in the afternoon, but I could swing an early dinner." I had committed to not eat after 7:00

PM because I was on this new fitness journey and I had lost 23 pounds to date. I had never been heavy, but she was concerned about my heart health because high blood pressure plagued me for years. Because of this new regimen, I was no longer on Atenenol for my hypertension, and I was feeling better than I had since the 1980s. We agreed to meet at Darden Grill.

"Perfect." He said. "I'll see you then. Have a good night, friend." *Friend?* Did he just call me FRIEND! What a fool I must be. Here I am, prancing around like some teenager, getting butterflies in my stomach over a man, and he is only interested in being my friend. I had half a mind to call him back and tell him that I had enough friends, and I didn't need another one. I didn't need anything. I mentally retreated back into my reality. Widow. Old. Lonely. Fit. Free. I had committed to go to dinner with a man that wasn't attracted to me. Or was he? How would I ever know? Those days seem to have long past, and I had to snap out of the idea that things could be different. I was very attracted to Glenn, but who was I to have those kinds of feelings? Good Lord. I had lost myself in the abyss of Millennial chatter among Nia and her friends and made the mistake of believing that I could have a life after Sam's death. Did I need to stay in my lane and simply live in quiet reflection, succumbing to the whims of my child and grandchild, and playing bingo at St. Peter's Catholic Church on Friday nights? I had no business dating or loving again.

Darden Grill was a family-owned restaurant that was managed by an old friend of Corrine's. Jocelyn Darden was a sweet woman who was raising six sons as a single mother. Her husband had disappeared under mysterious circumstances several years ago and she spent quite a bit of time in an institution grieving his disappearance and learning how to deal with her tremendous loss. James' stepping in to help her was a departure from his job as the lead investigator in her husband's case. Corrine didn't like it at all, though she would never say so in public. He always felt a tremendous sense of guilt that he couldn't solve the case. Joey had to be declared dead so that Jocelyn and the boys would receive the proceeds from Joey's life insurance policy. After the dust had settled, she took the life insurance money that she was awarded, quit her job as a school nurse, and opened Darden Grill with her sons. It had always been a dream of Joey's to open a restaurant, but with six boys to feed, his dreams were put on hold. Every chance I get, I try to support her. Because of Joey's disappearance, Jocelyn created a wall of resources that included everything from business cards of hair braiders to affirmations and inspirational quotes, prayer requests and words of encouragement. It was her way of honoring Joey's commitment to Hilbrand and it had become a community staple. Waiting to be seated was a joy since the wall was like a news magazine for patrons.

At 5:30 PM I hopped into the shower to begin the hour-long regime to get ready for my meetings with Glenn. Meetings. Funny how I called them meetings. I always pulled out my best lingerie or doubled up on my trusted coconut oil for a "meeting." I wanted to look and feel my best. I stepped my naked body into the shower and got a glimpse of my backside in the mirror. I could see how my time at the gym and my clean eating was benefiting me. I was by no means a brick house, but I wasn't a she shed either. My body was changing, but more than anything, my mind was opening up to the idea that I may be in love with someone other than Sam. I tingled at the thought.

There is nothing more satisfying than the first moments of a hot shower. How the droplets of water burn your skin just a bit. The way your body acclimates to the temperature, and how the flow covers your skin in a cascade. I had purchased some bath gel from Gentry's Bath House that was supposed to "make your skin feel like silk." I'm not sure if the claims were accurate. All I know is that this was a far cry from my childhood where you washed your body with the same soap that washed your hair, the laundry, and the dishes.

I squeezed a dollop of the Vanilla Gelee gel onto my loofah and watched as the suds formed. I thought about how Nia and her girlfriends spoke so freely about abandoning their loofahs during a shower and using their hands to wash instead. They talked about feeling their body and embracing every curve and bump. I scrubbed my skin and allowed the water to rinse me clean. Before I began my second sudsing, I gently stepped out of the shower to make sure the door was locked. I didn't want Nia barging in as she had done so many times before. I was about to do something that I had never done, and I didn't need an audience.

For my second wash, I drizzled the gel onto my hand. The sensation of rubbing my hands together gave me a strange sense of shame. I hadn't really touched my body in years. Who does? Especially at my age. I moisturize every day, but Nia and her friends talked about having intention when you touch your skin. They made the experience sound liberating and exhilarating. Nia and her friends have a freedom and self-awareness that I simply lacked. Chalk it up to age. My generation didn't have that level of freedom or a forum to discuss how they felt about their bodies, sexuality, or intimate feelings. Those that did explore women's sexuality were deemed immoral or worse, hippies. I decided to take the leap into what Nia's friends had spoken so openly about. I closed my eyes and rubbed the slick gel on my arms and legs, behind, and stomach. I felt my body for the first time in...well...forever. My skin was slick, and I could feel the muscles that were forming beneath the surface. My breasts hung gently against my chest. I felt them for the first time since the children were babies. They had nourished my children, been toys for Sam, and filled out dresses, but I discovered that they were so much more than that. They were an extension of my body that was designed for utility *and* **my** pleasure. I fell in love with them in that moment. I felt the ripples of the skin on my arms and the muscles in my legs. I caressed myself and sought to honor every bit of me with a gentle, intentional touch. I stopped short when I got to my pelvis. I wasn't able to graduate to wash my vagina with my hands yet. It still felt like a forbidden area for exploration. I wasn't ready to touch myself *THERE* with my bare hands. Nia and her friends called that a "happy ending" to a hot shower. I had to grow to be able to find my "happy place."

I rinsed my body for a second time and opened my eyes after the waterfall had drained from the faucet. There was something about that self-exploration that gave me confidence and made me feel sexier than I had since my days in Rome. As always, I stepped out of the shower and promptly slathered my body with coconut oil. With my newfound confidence and desire to know my body, I didn't miss one inch of my skin. It was purposeful moisturization. I wrapped myself in my white robe and stood in my closet looking for just the right outfit. I settled on a pair of I-899s that were light blue, and a red blouse. Sam always said that I looked good in red. I began thinking about what he would think about me meeting with Glenn. I wondered if I should even go ahead with another "meeting" at all. I hung the red blouse back in my closet and sat on the side of my bed contemplating whether I should go or not. Just then, my phone rang, "Heeeyyyy

Gram. Are you getting ready for another meeting?" It was Nia.

"Hi sweetheart." I responded. "Yes. Me and Glenn are getting together for an early dinner and the Darden Grill." I could hear her giggle when I was speaking, "Well, have fun. Do you have condoms Gram? I see how Glenn looks at you and you may want to be prepared." Horrified, I said, "Listen little girl, me and Glenn are just friends! I have no intention on sleeping with anyone. Plus, I'm 73 and he's going on 75. I don't think that's even a possibility physically. I'd mess around and slip a disk and he'd dislocate his hip and then we would end up on the news after being found stuck together." We both laughed hysterically. I didn't tell Nia that Glenn wasn't interested in me in that way. I didn't want any more Millennial relationship advice.

"Well, call me after dinner...or breakfast." Nia snickered.

"Bye granddaughter!" I hung up the phone and shook my head. I wondered if he is a Trojan man or a Magnum kinda guy? Well, it didn't matter. He was just a friend.

When I arrived at Darden Grill, I found Glenn standing in front of the wall reading some of the posts. I stood behind him and said, "This wall has everything on it." He turned slowly, gave me a once over.

"Not everything."

I blushed. *We are just friends.* We embraced and made pleasantries. He was dressed in a white linen button-down shirt and black pants. He wore a silver Cubanlink bracelet that rested on his dark brown wrist. It never rattled. The bracelet was large and almost cartoonlike. He wore no other jewelry. I noticed that his left ring finger bore no indication that he had ever worn a wedding band.

Weeks earlier, after a workout, we had stopped at the Banana Split for another smoothie. We sat on the wood slat bench outside the main entrance and chatted about our lives and our families. He told me that his wife, Gail, had up and left him 7 years ago. She claimed that she was sick of his womanizing ways, but soon after their split, before the ink was dry on the divorce settlement, Gail had moved to a small Florida town with her "caretaker" Dax who was 30 years her junior. Glenn spoke in a scripted way.

"I wasn't always a saint in our marriage. I strayed, she stayed. Those exploits were years ago, and I was dedicated to her and our family. After our last daughter graduated from college, Gail began to change. She was distant and cold and one day, I came home, and she was gone."

Glenn said that she had left a note saying that she needed to have a life that wasn't defined by her marital status or status as a mother. She wanted to be free to be her full self, and she didn't think she could do that within the confines of marriage. Weeks later, she served him divorce papers and that was it. He spoke of the devastation and embarrassment that her unceremonious departure with the "caretaker" had been. No one empathized with him because he had a playboy reputation in the community. Whether he ever made good on all of the advances that he made toward women, or that were made toward him, is unknown, but he freely expressed how, in 1987, he had had an affair with a woman that worked in his office. He regretted that indiscretion and remained faithful to Gail from that point forward. He had regrets. He wanted me to believe that he was fine with his marriage being the source of snide comments and side looks by his buddies, but I could see that he was embarrassed and hard pressed to tap into the feelings of shame and regret that lay at the surface of his bronze skin.

Their marriage, according to Glenn, was the talk of the town at the time, and each new sordid detail of Gail and her "caretaker" was on full display for all to consume. They were the "it" couple in Shelton, a town that neighbored Hilbrand. Glenn and Gail had the perfect looking relationship, and although I had obviously never met them, their names graced the society pages of our local newspaper for years. He was a prominent partner in a law firm, and she was a school administrator at Shelton Academy, a private high school for academically gifted students. They ran in the right circles and had influence and access in Shelton. Their three daughters, I learned, were just as *perfect* as their marriage appeared to be. Each one of his daughters had gone off to prestigious HBCUs, all earning master's degrees. They were successful and, by all accounts, unaffected by their parent's situation. From the outside looking in, everything was wonderful, but Glenn spoke of the undercurrent of infidelity and mistrust that came bubbling over when he and Gail divorced. I'd be lying if I said that his cheating didn't bother me. Sam had been faithful, from what I knew, and I had always been disgusted by the idea of a cheating spouse.

I glanced down at my own hand and noticed that my ring tan was still fading. I thought for sure that the indentation that rested on my finger would last forever, but it didn't. When I took my wedding ring off on that first anniversary after Sam's death, my skin instantly began to fill up again. I suppose my heart and soul did too.

I turned my gaze back to Glenn. His skin glowed and I could see the outline of his pectoral muscles through his shirt. Glenn always dressed well and his clothes fit him like they were custom made for his body. It was effortless. He wore a signature fragrance that smelled like teakwood. It was fresh and intoxicating.

"You look beautiful. And may I say, you are WEARIN' those jeans!" I blushed inside and thanked Glenn for the compliment. My body, before beginning with Nia, was not one that was easily poured into them, even if they were larger in size. There was something about the unforgiving structure of denim that my body didn't appreciate. I needed stretch in the fabric and a little give in the waistband. My I-899s fit beautifully and I looked fit and felt fabulous.

The hostess called Glenn's name, and we were directed to a table right next to the back windows that overlooked the lake. It was the perfect setting for a meeting. We were seated right at 7:00 PM as the sun was just beginning to set. White, floor length tablecloths were used during the dinner hour and tapered candles were lit to enhance the warmth and beauty of the setting. Jocelyn had done an amazing job designing the restaurant. It was warm and woodsy, but not cliché.

We sat down and Glenn asked about my day.

"After class I just went home and chatted with Nia. I had to run some errands and of course, I showered."

"Tell me about that." Glenn said.

"About what?" Here we go, I thought. He's doing it again! Flirting without *flirting*. There is no way this man wants me to give him a play by play of my shower.

"What do you want to hear about Glenn?" I said with annoyance in my voice. Glenn put his hand up as if to block the darts that were shooting from my eyes.

"Your errands. What did you have to do?" He was stunned that I had given him such an attitude. He sat back in his chair, "Listen…I just like your company. I think you're attractive and I really would like to get to know you even better. I am just looking for someone genuine to spend my time with. You are a wonderful lady and I think that we could build a great friendship. You are beautiful, but I don't want to move too fast and I shouldn't have kissed you after the Banana Split." I felt awful. Who was I to think that he wanted anything more than a chess partner, or someone to walk in the park with and feed the ducks? Plus, I wasn't interested in being another notch on his already tarnished belt. I had to stop listening to Nia who had convinced me that I could live a new life of adventure and sex and intimacy with Glenn. No. I was a 73-year-old widow who needed to remember that my best days were behind me and that all of that other stuff was for young people. If Glenn wanted a friend, then a friend he would get. *But, like Livy....a had needs...*

Feeling ashamed and incredibly vulnerable, I snapped out of my own thoughts and said, "I understand. Let's just order."

I decided on the Cobb Salad. Glenn chose baked chicken with roasted red potatoes and green beans. We ate our meal in virtual silence. I was embarrassed that I ever thought that this could be anything romantic. Why had I let my imagination run wild? I really enjoyed Glenn's company and I didn't want to jeopardize our friendship with my fantastical teenage crush. During dinner, there was the occasional comment about the weather or how the lights of the harbor looked beautiful against the lake. But more than anything, there was a tension that I couldn't explain, and all I wanted to do was go home, curl up in my robe and watch the night's episode of *Family Feud* that I had asked Nia to tape for me on my TV. After clearing our dinner dishes, the waitress asked if we wanted anything else. Before I could answer, Glenn said, "I'd like a cup of coffee. Would you like something?"

Begrudgingly I said, "Hot tea with lemon and honey please."

What I really wanted to say was, *"Glenn, I really want to go home because I hate ducks and I've never learned how to play chess. At first, I felt like a fool for thinking that I am a real woman who has a space and place in her heart to love again. I thought that I was just an old, widowed woman who is slick with coconut oil and full of salad. But now, Glenn, I want you, all of you."* But I stayed silent, trying to gather my thoughts so that I could tell him how I really felt. My life had been a series of reactions. I was taught that women were to react, not respond, or even initiate. Now, those days were over! Nia and her friends were living their lives on their terms and it was high time for me to do the same. I needed to tell Glenn that **I** wanted him!

Our beverages arrived at the table and Glenn, after dressing his coffee with two creams, one sugar, stopped mid-stir and looked at me. *OK, Doris...say what you want to say! You have spent your entire life waiting to be heard. If you want him, say so! What have you got to lose?* I opened my mouth to speak, but Glenn spoke first.

"I lied to you." I looked up from my steaming cup of tea.

"About what?" I asked. The honey pot was to my left. He sat up straight and composed himself. I gathered a dollop of honey on the swizzle stick to put in my teacup.

"I am very fond of you. I really like you and I am very attracted to you Doris. I'm just afraid of that though, because we are two people who have already loved and lost, for so long." Glenn leaned in, and in a soft tone he said, "I am afraid to love again because I am afraid to lose again."

I stared in his eyes, and I could see his sincerity. The truth is, I was afraid too. I loved Sam so much that I never thought I would ever feel that kind of love, and I wasn't sure I had permission to, but damn, this man was moving me in ways that I never thought possible.

"Glenn, let's just take things slow. We have both lived well and we have everything to live for now. I am fond of you and there's no reason to put labels on what we are doing here." *Oh, and let's get the hell outta here so that I can get some of that good-good!*

I was exhausted at the thought of a relationship, but intrigued at the same time. My head was swirling. Just then, a small drop of honey fell on my index finger. In the middle of my soliloquy, I dabbed my napkin in my water to rub off the honey. Before I could, Glenn grabbed my hand, looked deep in my eyes, took my index finger, and gently placed it in his mouth. Our eyes were locked as he sucked the honey from my finger. I could feel the magic of his tongue at work. His mouth was warm and wet, and my body was too. My jeans began to tighten, and I was responding to his artistry. I hadn't felt this way in years, decades, ever. I slowly came out of the hypnotic rhythms of his tongue, and the deep stare of his eyes to mine. Finally, coming to my senses, I scanned the room for our waitress, waved my other hand, motioning for her to come to the table. She nodded, and looked our way.

I spoke breathlessly, "Check please."

12

In A Sentimental Mood

You remember what it felt like when you were a teenager and the boy or girl you like told you that they liked you back? Remember that flutter in your stomach? Well, I thought at this age, the flutters were dead. No indeed! They existed and they came into full bloom when that man put my sweet finger in his mouth. We walked out of the restaurant with no plan in mind. My body had unlocked, and I awaited Glenn to enter. He held my hand as we traversed the parking lot.

I spoke first, "Thank you for…well…a lovely evening. It was… well lovely. What's next on your agenda? Would you like to come over for a nightcap?"

He leaned over me, "I would love to." I gave him my address and he said that he'd be there shortly. He had to run home to take care of his beloved Jack Russel Terriers, Ashford and Simpson.

He opened my car door and as I sat down searching for my seatbelt, he leaned in and kissed me gently on the corner of my mouth. It was quick, but sensuous. I closed my door, started the car, and immediately called Nia.

"Hey Gram," she said. "How was dinner?"

"Nia, Gram needs help. Glenn is coming over for a nightcap. What should I do?" I asked, nervously.

"A what? First of all, what's a nightcap? Is that old people lingo for Netflix and Chill?" Nia said with glee.

"Lord child…if your mother finds out I have this man in my house, I will never hear the end of it!"

"Well, Gram, join me in the doghouse! Mom keeps me there from time-to-time. There's plenty of room for you! Now listen, in all seriousness, have fun tonight. You deserve to have a little swang in your thang! Use protection, we don't need you popping up pregnant!" She laughed out loud, and I had to join in.

"Lord Nia! I'll call you later on tonight. Love you."

"Talk to you in the morning Gram."

I blushed and shook my head. *Morning?*

I parked my car in the driveway and walked up to the front door. I had been through that front door millions of times, but this time, it felt different. I was about to invite a man into the home that me and Sam had built 43 years ago using his GI Bill. *What was I doing?* This has to be a sin or violation of some marriage rule. Surely, the fornication was going to send me to Hell and with the sexual thoughts that I had for Glenn, I was already halfway there. I peeled myself out of my jeans and blouse to prepare to freshen up. With a spray of perfume, a swipe with a warm, damp washcloth, I was refreshed. I slid into a loose-fitting lounge outfit that I had purchased last month at Nordstrom during their Half Yearly Sale. It wasn't sexy, but it was soft and clung to my body in the right way. It looked effortless. It was comfortable and non-assuming. I didn't want to seem eager. I checked the clock, and it was 8:55 PM. Five more minutes and my doorbell would be ringing, and on the other side of the door would stand a new man, a new life, a new love, and an amazing tongue. At 9:00 PM on the dot, my cell phone rang. It was Glenn.

"Hi. So, I am making my way for that nightcap, but I'm running a bit late. Turns out, my daughter had a leak in her house, and I have been calling all over the city for a hotel room for her. There's some convention in town. I think we may have to postpone tonight."

Glenn's youngest daughter lived in Rustil which was 45 minutes north. It was in the country, and to get there, you had to pass through some very small towns with questionable residents.

"I have to pass your house to get on the Interstate. Perhaps I can swing by when I leave Rustil. It will be late, but…"

"I understand, but I don't think that's a good idea." I said begrudgingly.

"Yes. I think you're probably right," he said. "Too much, too soon." The silence was deafening.

I could feel the tension through the phone and blurted out, "You know Glenn, I do have an extra bedroom if you are too tired from the late-night drive and *really* need a place to stay. It's got its own bathroom and everything. Very private. You're welcomed to stay. I don't mind."

Before the sentence fully left my mouth, I wanted to take it back. It was one thing to have a drink and trade a kiss, but it was an entirely different thing to have him spend the night. *Did I sound desperate?*

"I don't think *that's* a good idea. I can take the trip to Rustil tonight and then, perhaps, we can meet for lunch tomorrow," he said.

"That's probably a better idea anyway," I said. "Just call me when you get settled and we can schedule lunch."

"OK. Well, goodnight, Doris."

"Goodnight, Glenn."

I hung up the phone and an emptiness crept in. I had gotten my hopes up, only to be disappointed and showed my cards to boot. I was excited to see him and to possibly *SEE* him, but my dreams of intimacy with Glenn were dashed. Perhaps it was the universe's way of putting the kibosh on my teenage-like fantasy. I snapped back into myself and remembered that all this talk of living my best life was nonsense. I had no business trying to live like Nia and her friends. I should be knitting or going to club meetings, not pining after some man that wasn't my husband. I took off my lounge outfit, and threw it in the corner of my closet, slipped on my housecoat, my satin bonnet, and let Steve Harvey's "survey said" rock me to sleep.

I don't know how long I was asleep when suddenly, I heard my phone ring.

"Hello?" I answered with a groggy voice.

"Hi Doris. It's me."

"Glenn? What time is it?"

"About 11:00 PM. Did I wake you?" I wanted to say, *"YES dammit! It's 11:00 PM"* Instead I said, "Yes, I've been asleep for a while and it's very late. I assume you made it home? Let's talk in the morning."

Glenn chimed in, "So I didn't make it anywhere. I've been outside your door since 9:30 PM trying to find a way to call you and tell you that...I want you. Tonight. In my arms. In your bed." I sat straight up from my sleeping position. *Was I dreaming?*

"What?"

"Open the door, Doris."

I popped off the couch and walked gingerly to the front door. I peeked through the peephole and there he stood, looking handsome and focused. I looked down to unlock the door and saw that I was wearing my old housecoat. I felt my head, and discovered the satin bonnet perched atop my messy bun. I panicked.

"Uh, Glenn? Can you give me a minute?"

"No," he said. "If I don't see you in the next second...Doris, open the door." His voice was different. Long gone was the sweet flirtatiousness that I had grown accustomed to. This time, he was serious. I clicked the lock and the door flung open.

He walked into the house, sat his bag on the floor, closed the door and kissed me. His mouth tasted sweet, and his lips were soft and supple. I pulled away for a moment to assess his eyes. They were open and fixed on me. He walked me to the couch without saying a word. He sat next to me.

"Doris, I want you to know that I am not the man I used to be."

"OK." I was nervous because I didn't know what he was trying to convey.

"My life, as a young man, was filled with a quest to collect notches on my belt. When I met Gail and we fell in love, I traded my belt for a noose."

"OK."

"Our marriage was happy for about a year, and then we started to have children and the stress of keeping up was too much. She became bitter and started stepping out of our marriage and I tried to stay faithful, but I failed."

"Glenn, why are you telling me this?" I asked because none of that mattered to me. We all have a past and it's what makes us who we are.

Glenn turned his body to mine. We were face-to-face.

"I'm telling you this because I haven't felt like this in years. You're special and I don't know if I can be the man that you want, even though I am willing to do whatever I can to be. I don't want to hurt you, Doris, and I don't want to be hurt either. I have the scars of infidelity on my heart, and I have wielded the knife and caused my ex-wife's too."

That's grown ass man talk. When you're a fully realized adult, you are free to speak your truth without apology or shame. I leaned and kissed him gently on the corner of his mouth.

"Have enough courage to trust love one more time and always one more time." He said.

"Maya Angelou?" I smiled inside.

"Yes. Her writings and poetry are some of my favorites. You have to know that we are in control of how we love. I'm here, right now, with you."

It was my turn to speak my own truth.

"Glenn?" I touched his hand. "There's a lot on my mind. I am not the woman that my husband married. I'm not sure who I am. For women, our identities are often determined by the roles that we live." I continued. "For so long, I performed, but I have decided to live my life for me and do what I want to do."

"Is that why you invited me here for a nightcap?" He slid closer to me on the sofa and brushed my leg with his hand. "Am I what you want to do?"

My heart began to quicken.

"I…I…" I stuttered trying to get my words out. Glenn stood up and pulled his phone from his pocket. He fumbled with the screen. Moments later, I heard the sound. From the speaker, John Coltrane's tenor saxophone played *In A Sentimental Mood*. Originally composed by Duke Ellington, it is arguably the sexiest song ever written. It's snare drum piano riffs mimic all the good of a night of passion. It's playful, sensual, and hypnotic.

Glenn offered me his hand, and I joined him, standing. Our fingers intertwined as the music play. We swayed until the song ended. Just as the snare drum offered its final goodbye, Glenn laid my limp body down on the sofa and another rendition began to play. Ella Fitzgerald's voice floated into my ear:

In a sentimental mood

I can see the stars come through my room

While your loving attitude

Is like a flame that lights the gloom

On the wings of every kiss

Drifts a melody so strange and sweet

In this sentimental bliss

You make my paradise complete

Rose petals seem to fall

It's all I could dream to call you mine

My heart's a lighter thing

Since you made this night a thing divine

In a sentimental mood

I'm within a world so heavenly for I never dreamt

That you'd be loving sentimental me

* * *

He knelt in front of me. His hand dragged slowly up my legs. The coolness of his bracelet chilled my hot body. Under my housecoat he reached my hips and pulled me closer to the edge of the couch. He gently rubbed my clitoris and I squealed. His tongue met his hand, and my body responded in a way that I had never felt, not even in Rome. John Coltrane revisited us and he brought *Psalm* with him.

Sam had never ventured into this realm with me. I assumed that he had his share of oral experience in the military, but I was an oral virgin, even after 50 years, 4 months, and 27 days of marriage. Glenn's masterful tongue took me into bliss and a rush of wet warmth streamed from my now tense, then limp body. He stood up and guided me into my bedroom. He had never been to my home, but he seemed to know exactly where our night would culminate. The lights were off in the room, and I could feel him wrestling with the wall to find the switch.

"I want to see you, all of you. Where is the switch?" He said.

Having the lights on was foreign to me. I lived and loved in darkness. Hell, it was even dark in Rome! This. Was. New. There's no hiding in the light. I flipped the switch on the wall and there he stood, erect and shirtless. His pants were about to split, and my head was spinning. This was better than Rome. This was intimacy at its finest. Soft and slow. Sincere, he guided me toward him.

He undressed himself. I watched how he was as effortless taking off his clothes as I imagined he would be putting them on. It felt as though he was peeling the layers of his past hurts and pains and leaving them on the ground, no longer needed to protect is soul. No struggle, just a smooth sliding of his pants and boxer briefs. He stood, unashamed, in the light. His body was beautiful. Vulnerable. He continued to stare into my eyes as he began unzipping my housecoat. I didn't have time to be embarrassed at the state of my attire. *Was I ready to be completely seen?* I was hypnotized by his eyes, and he reassured me, without saying a word, that I was safe. I surrendered to him in my silence that the path that he was on was welcomed. He opened the coat and for the first time since opening the door, he broke his gaze from my eyes. He studied my body and looked as though he was making mental notes. I felt a cold rush of air and breathed in deeply. I was free.

"You are beautiful." He said. "I have wanted you since the first moment I laid eyes on you Doris."

I blushed and said, "Glenn...I'm scared, but I have never wanted anyone more than I want you."

I couldn't believe that those words came out of my mouth. Nia and her friends taught me that I needed to say what I wanted and never apologize for it. The Millennials are blunt and outspoken, to say the least. Glenn wasn't shocked, rather, he softened his gaze. He looked into my eyes again and said, "I'm in the business of giving you what you want." He caressed my breasts, kissed me, and gently poured his body into mine. His erect penis rested inside of me as we moved rhythmically together. He pulled his chest away from mine and looked into my eyes again. Mine were closed.

"Open your eyes, Doris. I'm not behind your lids, I'm right here." With our bodies in sync, I opened my eyes and for the first time, I saw love.

I loved Sam, but I don't think I was ever *in love* with him. I always felt like an accessory with Sam, but with Glenn looking into my eyes he fell deeper and deeper inside of me, and it felt like my pleasure, my wants, my needs, were all that he cared about. Me. I mattered, first. He didn't speak another word, and neither did I. Ours was a silent communication of breaths, moans, and tender touch. He waited for me, and we rode the wave of ecstasy together. I was exhausted and tingling all over. With Sam, I was used to him collapsing on top of me in exhaustion after he climaxed. Glenn gently released himself, walked to the bathroom, and returned with a warm, damp cloth. He wiped the sweat from my naked, exposed body. I tingled when he got to my "happy ending." He watched me and smiled sweetly. I wanted to cry. *How had I lived this long and never felt this way?* No one, not even Givano, had touched me so deeply. He leaned down and kissed me on the corner of my mouth, covered our bodies with the white comforter as I rested my head on his chest. The rise and fall of his breathing began to lull me to sleep. I shed a single tear remembering Sam.

As if on cue, sensing my thoughts, Glenn held me closer and whispered, "I supposed it's OK to love again…and I…I love you, Doris."

I drew closer, "I love you too, Glenn."

With that, I fell asleep with a king in my queen.

13

Hiding in Plain Sight

That first encounter with Glenn changed me. I mean I was transformed. All I could think about was him. His smell. His body. His kiss. His touch. Glenn was bigger and better than Rome in every sense. He was magical and majestic. Our lovemaking was all I could think about. It wasn't the intercourse part that moved me, but the level of intimacy that Glenn and I had developed. It was pure and easy and passionate. We spoke on the phone everyday, and saw each other most nights. Our workouts were becoming less strenuous because our bedroom escapades were creating quite the burn. We would lay with each other almost every night, and wake in each others arms each morning. Much to my discomfort, he had even gotten a little more expressive in public. I wanted to maintain an "in-house" type of relationship, but Glenn wanted to take our love on the road. Hilbrand wasn't the kind of community that celebrated public displays of affection, especially for a woman of my age and station in life. Older couples were rarely seen hugging, or even holding hands. We were supposed to fade in the background and allow the foreground to be occupied by those without an *AARP* card. Also, I was raised in a family where kissing or embracing in public was considered vulgar and inappropriate. I would often shoo Glenn's hand away when he tried to hold them and, even though the honey sucking was wonderful, I was horrified at his blatant display in public. *What if someone saw us?* I thought. *How would I deal with the backlash?*

"Doris, I know you want to keep us under wraps, but I want to shout **US** from the roof tops." Glenn would often say.

"In due time, Glenn." I reassured him. Even though it had been over a year since Sam's death, I still felt like I was cheating on him. I was living the shift that Dara had encouraged me to live, but I would be lying if I said that I was fully invested in this new life.

I was stretching one morning when my phone rang. It was Glenn.

"Hello?"

"Be ready to go in 10 minutes." The line went dead before I could ask for details.

I looked at the display on my phone in disbelief. *He hung up on me!*

"Oh no!" My fingers started dialing his number, when my phone rang again.

"Um, hello? Are we hanging up on people now?" I said in my sassiest voice.

"You're funny. Listen, dress comfortably...maybe those jeans that I like. Better yet, wear something that you can take off easily... you never know when the mood will strike. You have 8 minutes." The phone clicked off again.

He's gone crazy.

I stood up and walked to my closet. I scanned my clothes and decided on a flowing swing-dress and a pair of ankle boots.

After a quick, but thorough 2-minute shower, I emerged from the steamy space to find Glenn standing, naked. I was startled. "Glenn! How did you get in here." He smiled and walked me to the kitchen.

Without saying a word, Glenn lifted me up on the island. The cold granite caused a chilly jolt through my body. He laid me flat on my back.

"Close your eyes, Doris."

I obliged. I trusted Glenn and I had never been disappointed when he was in this type of mood. I wondered what would come next. A warm cloth, or a full-body massage. Either way, I was ready. Just as I was about to open my eyes with curiosity, I felt the chill of an ice cube on my thigh. *Holy shit.* The sensation was ridiculous. It was truly better than anything that I had ever felt. He dragged the cube from one end of my body to the other. He was a master of seduction and he used something as simple as an ice cube to bring me to the brink of pure ecstasy. He reached down and kissed me as I lay with the chill of the ice cube resting on my flesh. He traced the shape of by breasts with his mouth and when I reached for his body, I realized that he was standing behind my head. *Hot damn, an upside down kiss?* I was so lost in his artistry that I didn't hear the click of the door lock.

"Hey Gram…It's…OH MY GOD!!!"

I popped up from the island and Glenn and I tried to cover our naked bodies with whatever we could find. My breasts, with a dish towel and my bottom with an oven mitt. I looked over at Glenn who had concealed his erect penis with a pot.

"Ummmm…so…I'm gonna go." Nia was speechless. "Umm… yeah…so…I'll talk to you later, Gram. Bye Mr. Glenn. Good to see…I mean…nice to see…I mean…yeah, so bye." Nia dashed out of the house in a flash. I looked at Glenn in horror. "Lord Glenn! What are we doing?" He looked under the pot.

"Not much now."

We shamefacedly retreated to the bedroom. Silent, we put on our clothes on. I could barely look at him. "Hungry," I asked.

"Yeah."

"Let's go to dinner." Glenn suggested a small Chinese restaurant located in downtown Hilbrand called Hunan.

We climbed into his Lexus Coupe and made our way to Hunan, in silence. I didn't think I would ever recover from the embarrassment of my granddaughter watching me get *iced* on the kitchen island.

We sat down and it felt like everyone was looking at us. Hunan was an open grill restaurant that prepared your dinner in front of you at your table. The experience was one-part entertainment, and one-part dinner preparation. We needed the distraction. With Nia walking in on us, I felt ashamed and embarrassed. Sensing my discomfort, and attempting to make me laugh, Glenn reached down, grabbed my thigh and asked the waiter for extra ice. I couldn't help but laugh. The tension was broken.

"Jesus, that child is going to be scarred for life."

"Do you think she *saw*…me?" Glenn asked. "I was behind you so maybe I was covered enough where she didn't *see*…me."

"By the way that Nia ran out of the house, I'm pretty sure she saw all of you…and me."

We looked at each other and laughed.

Out of the corner of my eye I could see 3 people looking our way. I squinted. "Oh God." I said nervously.

"What is it?" Glenn asked.

"Some of the Highlands are here." *God, please don't let them see me. Please don't let them*...Just then I hear the voice of Gina Taylor, Rochelle Green, and that busybody, Cecily Halistair.

"Doris...is that you?" Cecily squealed.

"Oh hi ladies. Been a long time. How are you?" These women weren't even looking at me. They kept their eyes focused on Glenn. Without waiting for an answer, Gina said, "I'm Gina, Gina Taylor, and you are?"

Glenn stood up, "I'm Gle..."

"Glenn Spears. You are THAT Glenn Spears." Cecily said. "Oh we *know* who you are." The trio gave each other a look.

"Yes, this is Glenn Spears." I chimed in. "Glenn and I are friends, out having a friendly dinner, as friends, because we are...well, friends." Everyone was looking at me in disbelief. I had said too much. My attempt at remaining cool failed.

Gina, Cecily, and Rochelle watched as I fumbled my words and tried to act as though this man hadn't just used an ice cube to make me squeal with delight hours earlier. "Uh huh. Well, it's nice to have friends these days." Cecily said snidely. "Well, we will leave you to enjoy your *friendly* dinner."

Glenn stood again, "It was a pleasure to meet you all."

Rochelle spoke softly, "The pleasure was all ours. Night-night, Dor."

I waved slightly as they walked away.

I looked at Glenn in disbelief. "Well, there goes our privacy. It just walked out the door because those three have a larger audience than *The Wall Street Journal*."

"You act like that's a bad thing. Are we doing this or just *doing it*?" I could sense Glenn's annoyance. I reached for his hand and he pulled away from me.

"Glenn."

He turned his head away from me.

"I told you before, Doris, that I was in this for the long haul. I'm not going to be your little secret. Either you want all of me, or you get none of me. I have been hurt too much in my life already and I am not interested in playing games."

"I'm not playing games. I just…Glenn…Sam just died, and…"

"Doris, he's gone!" He looked me directly in my eyes. "I'm here now. I am here, with YOU, right now. Either you want me or you don't. I'm all in. All in Doris Ashworth. Where are you?"

I looked around the room and saw no other familiar faces. Everyone was staring at us, or at least, that's how I saw the people in the room. It felt like everyone knew that we were lovers and that I was a widow sleeping with a divorcée. I wore my own, self-imposed scarlet letter. I excused myself to go to the restroom. Looking at myself in the mirror, I tried to gather my emotions.

"Get it together, Doris." *Get busy living or get busy dying.* I wanted to live and I wanted so desperately not to care about what everyone thought about my life. I must have been in the restroom for a while, because when I returned to the table, Glenn was gone. The hostess told me that he had paid the bill and that he had called a car to take me home. I was shocked. *He left me.* I was too hurt to be angry.

I thanked the hostess and walked out of Hunan, to climb into a waiting Uber Black. The driver, Yusef, spoke softly with a heavy

British accent.

"Mr. Spears left you a message. It is on the seat. We should be at your home in 15 minutes."

I reached for a white piece of paper that was folded in half, on the seat next to me.

Doris,

This is not how this night was supposed to go. When you're ready to love me the way that I love you, out loud, unapologetic, and in public, I'll be right there waiting for you.

Glenn

Had I lost him because I was afraid? And what was I afraid of? On the drive home, I replayed the events of the evening, and my mind began racing. *How did I get here?* I thought about my whole life with Sam and Corrine, Nia, Rome, all of it. I wanted to be free. *But free from what? My thoughts? My burdens? Expectations?* Being with Glenn was all I wanted. No. Being free was all I wanted. I thought that he was the source of my freedom. But as the streetlights illuminated my broken ideas, I realized that I was alone and he couldn't be my source. In that moment, I knew that I had it wrong. I need to be my own source of freedom, and there was no way that I could ever be free until I got honest with myself and told my truth. I realized that I had been living a lie for 50 years, 4 months, and 27 days. Worse than that, that woman, that dishonest, unfulfilled woman had raised a daughter, Corrine, and now, my daughter was hiding from her own truth. She, in turn, raised Nia, my granddaughter, who was the unfortunate beneficiary of decades of women living in shame and harvesting fields of lies. She, in fact, was the by-product of lies, and I had started the cycle in motion the moment I traded my soul for doing what was right, and what was expected of me. It was time to attack the elephants in the room, and I had to start with the biggest one. The one that Corrine created and that, I, unbeknownst to her, helped her conceal. Until the secrets of our collectives lives were revealed, I was never going to be able to live freely, in my new life. It was time. Now.

14

Picture Perfect

As I was thinking about cleaning out Sam's things from the closet, Corrine was cleaning out her own closet and discovered that skeletons never *really* go away.

"Can you believe it's been so long since Daddy's been gone?"

Corrine asked James as they sat at the kitchen table eating their traditional Tuesday dinner of salmon, white rice, and broccoli. The sound of *CNN* blared in the background as James listened partly to what Corrine was saying, but more so to Anderson Cooper.

"I just can't believe he's gone." Corinne said.

Again, James offered a small grunt as he took a bite of his salmon. Their small talk had been reduced to simple sounds. Both Corrine and James were living separate lives in private. Sure, their public lives were the picture of perfection, but behind closed doors, they lived more like roommates than husband and wife.

They met when Corrine returned home to Hilbrand after graduation. They both attended the University of Michigan, but they didn't know each other in college. Corrine had been hired as a field correspondent for *KNFD*, a news station in Nelford, a neighboring city, just 40 miles north of Hilbrand. She was assigned to cover local social events and she could be found on the 5:00 PM news petting goats or riding roller coasters at the county fair. One day, she was on location at the annual Fourth of July parade and a handsome police cadet was hired to provide security to her and her camera man. James was a tall, handsome young man with a dazzlingly bright, white smile. The two spent all day together. While James stood watch, Corrine provided sound bites that would be used for the late night broadcast. By the end of the parade, they had exchanged phone numbers and arranged to go out to dinner the next night.

They dated for six-months before James proposed to Corrine. Sam and I approved of their union because James had a playful, yet calming affect on Corrine, and he had a stable career and family. Before James, Corrine would have never gone on a picnic in the park in the middle of the day or walked barefoot through the fountain in downtown Hilbrand. James brought out the best of her. She was relaxed and carefree and we welcomed the less pent up version of our daughter.

They were engaged for a year and then they got married. Their wedding was the talk of the town.

Handsome Police Officer Marries Television Darling

The headlines were everywhere. They were the "it" couple in Hilbrand. Corrine ate up the media attention and defaulted to her usual perfect appearances. Everyone who was anyone was invited to the wedding. It was covered by the news stations in Nelford and Hilbrand. The camera man at the reception interviewed Corrine, while James stood behind her with a closed mouth, Stepford smile plastered on his face. I remember watching James fade in the background at the reception. It was happening right before his very eyes. The real Corrine was emerging and her new husband was realizing that he was only an accessory in her life. Now, 30 years into a loveless marriage, they sat dutifully trying to stomach each other.

A year ago, James was on patrol in Hilbrand, West. Hilbrand is a quaint, beautiful city with railroad tracks that separate the haves and the have nots. East Hilbrand was for the haves. West, for the have nots. Our home is in the East. Well-appointed single-family homes with manicured lawns and luxury cars in the driveways dotted the East, while apartments and trailers peppered the West. The lush green grass of each house served as a welcome mat for young families and professionals. It is a multicultural community where everyone lives harmoniously. There are White families and Black families, Hispanic families, Asian families, Haitian families, and everyone in between. People from all walks of life live in Hilbrand. I'd never had one moment of discrimination living in there. It had always been welcoming to me and my family. Nia often mentions that there were times when she felt very much alone being only one of over a hundred African American children in her graduating class, but even with that, she was accepted, loved, and respected. Our political views are vast and varied, and rarely discussed. We, as a community, tend to lean moderately when discussing the economy, health care, or immigration.

The West and the East came together in collective sorrow several years ago when one of the bright lights in our community disappeared. Joseph Darden was a wonderful soul. He and his wife Jocelyn were the proud parents of five sons, with one on the way. Corrine had grown up with Jocelyn and Joseph, who everyone called Joey. His dream had always been to open a restaurant. During his high school years, when all the other boys were taking shop or car repair as an elective, Joey was in Home Economics learning the cook and sew a button on a dress. He got a good bit of teasing for his choices, but he was unmoved. He and Jocelyn were the talk of the town when she discovered that she was pregnant in their senior year of high school. Surprisingly, many in the community embraced this young couple and didn't make too much of a fuss over their situation. Many members of the Highlands had a lot to say about her virtue and their disgust that she hadn't "saved herself for marriage." I sat in our meetings listening to the hypocrisy of it all and wondered when the right time would be to mention my tryst in Rome.

Jocelyn and Joey married shortly after their first son was born. Two years after Ethan, came Even, Eron, Everette, Elijah, and Eric. All of the boys looked like Joey; pale, white skin, piercing ice blue eyes, and dark brown hair. They were striking. Jocelyn managed to maintain her girlish figure even after giving birth to all of those boys. Her thin frame and flawless olive complexion was the envy of women and the desire of men. Her features are distinct, but non-descript. She looks Middle Eastern, Italian, and Black all at the same time. There's was a beautiful union, until the day, that we believe Joey died.

The circumstances surrounding his death are steeped in mystery. No one knows how he died, or if he died at all. He disappeared shortly after Jocelyn announced her last pregnancy. James, now a detective, was the lead investigator in the search and he and his partner, Matt Madison, worked around the clock to solve his disappearance. They didn't find one shred of evidence. The investigation went from days to months, months to years until the court had to make a finding that he was to be declared legally dead. Jocelyn had 6 mouths to feed, no husband, all on a secretary's salary.

The insurance money that she received was a welcome relief to her and her children.

Corrine said that after the investigation yielded no results, James was different. He became quiet and withdrawn. He stopped going to his Friday happy hours with his friends and instead, spent his time carting the Darden boys back and forth to practices, recitals, and tutoring. He often had Nia and her "brothers" in his SUV while Corrine was at home waiting for he and Nia to come home. Secretly, Corrine resented the fact that James spent more time with Nia, the boys, and Jocelyn than with her. She made her disdain well-known to James almost nightly.

"I know she's a widow or whatever, but I'm your wife. You should be home with me." She often nagged.

"Doing what, Corrine? Talking about the latest drama with the Highlands, or your drama at work? That's all you seem to care about. You never ask me about anything." James retorted.

Their fighting wasn't new. In fact, when Nia was a child, she would drown out their arguments by taking a bath. The loud sound of the water hitting the tub was just enough to silence them for a while. She told me that she would fill the tub up, drain the water, just to fill it up again so she didn't have to hear them fight. The arguments, she said, usually lasted 3 fillings worth.

James and Corrine never considered divorce. They had to maintain the appearance of a happy marriage for the sake of Corrine's career as a local newscaster and her position in the Highlands. Appearances were everything to her. I couldn't blame her for how she thought or operated in the world. After all, she was my child. I raised her and much of who she is, is because of me. There were parts of Corrine, however, that I didn't understand. This need for perfection started after she came home from college. She was always particular about things, but it became an obsession for her after her sophomore year. Everything in her life appeared perfect, and when Nia was born, her obsession hit a fever pitch.

I thought it was strange when she and James bought their first home shortly before Nia was born. Corrine made quick work to change the interior and exterior of the house. White. Everything from the carpet to the walls, to the sofa, all of it was pure white. Sterile white. I remember mentioning my concern for her color choices given the fact that she was having a baby.

"Do you really think white is a good choice, Corrine. You *are* having a baby soon." I asked with concern in my voice.

"Mother, this baby is going to be different. She won't be like other babies. Don't worry." She'd respond with confidence.

How wrong she was. By the time Nia was 2, the white sofa had been painted, peed on, and punctured with a marker. Her dreams of having a perfect child were dashed when hurricane Nia made landfall. Nothing much had changed since those early days. I was soon going to be another stain on her perfect appearing life.

15

Everything in the dark may come to the light…

Corinne had a desire to be the best and always be seen in the light, even if, it was artificial light. In high school, she was the homecoming queen, class president, and all-around favorite student of most of the administration. She had her heart set on going to an Ivy League school after graduation. She decided that Journalism was going to be her field of study. As the editor of the yearbook the year that she graduated, she had been bitten by the journalism bug and was tasked with interviewing her classmates. She was involved with civic activities that me and her father had no knowledge of. She wasn't secretive, she told us just enough. As a youngster, she hid her high scoring essays and tests in her backpack. At the end of the semester, Corrine would have straight A's and then, unload a sea of 100% tests, quizzes, and assignments on us. It was overwhelming and amazing. She wanted huge triumphs rather than small victories. She was a star. We knew it from the moment that she was born, and we saw it, in its full glory the moment that she walked onto the campus at the University of Michigan.

She strutted on the green expanse like she owned it. We marveled at the brick buildings and the meticulous grounds. The university was beautiful. The look in Corrine's eyes told us that she believed that she belonged there. Sam and I were amazed at the order and organization of the campus. It was massive. Football stadium, here, basketball arena there. For me, it was overwhelming. Cheyney was a small place with tremendous history. It was the first HBCU in the country, although Sam and I would debate that fact on an almost daily basis.

When we entered Corinne's dorm room, we were met by a small slight shape, White girl with blonde hair. Her emerald eyes were striking. Her name was Helen, and she was from Billings, Montana. She was already in the room when we got there to drop off Corrine in her new home. Helen's parents had been there earlier in the afternoon and had already made their way back to Montana before we arrived. She said that her father was an executive for a box manufacturing company, and her mother was a stay-at-home mom. They had some event to attend the next evening and they had to return to Billings. I thought it strange that they had left her there, without any assistance or pomp and circumstance. In our family, the drop off during your first year of college was a ceremony of sorts. Helen sat on her bed as Sam, and I fussed over Corrine. We made her bed with the new linens that we had purchased and laid out all of her school supplies, including her new word processor and dot matrix printer that the church had gifted her the Sunday before we departed. I watched as Helen sat in awe of the dance that was happening before her eyes.

"Wow. All my parents left me with was $100 and a calling card." Helen said with her eyes wide staring at the color-coordinated throw pillows that Corrine arranged neatly on her bed.

We asked if she wanted to join us for dinner and she accepted our invitation. The four of us dined at a small Italian restaurant just South of campus. After dinner, we decided that it was best to go to the hotel and have Corrine and Helen go to their room. I had no reluctance of leaving Corrine that night. She was at home, and I knew that she was comfortable in her setting. About 10:00, later that evening, I received a call from Corrine from the pay phone at the end of her dorm hallway. It was a good idea to have gone to the bank earlier in the day to get her a roll of quarters.

"Mom? Helen is in there crying. What should I do?" She was speaking in a whisper. I told her to be supportive but allow Helen to cry it out.

"She's probably missing home. It's normal. She'll be fine in the morning."

I said gently, hoping to quell any fears that Corrine may have had about her roommate's state of mind. "Perhaps she should call her parents." I said.

"She did. They told her to grow up and then her mom hung up on her." I said some other comforting words that I don't remember and then offered Corrine a bit of sage advice, "Corrine, college is a microcosm of a city; there are people from all walks of life. You are going to have to learn how to take care of yourself, first. The issues that others have will work themselves out. You must stay focused."

I hoped that her college experience would be blissful, but something, deep down in my soul, told me that the next 4 years would be life altering, and she would never be the same. I was right. I didn't know then how drastic the change would be or how it would shape the rest of her life, but my Corrine left Michigan very different than how she had arrived.

During her junior year, Corinne was selected the assistant editor of the school newspaper. As a journalism major, she was beginning her career. She started as a field correspondent, then a copy editor, and now, the assistant editor. Though the newspaper was published at the university, it was a true periodical with a large, loyal readership. Corrine took her role very seriously. She had received accolades and awards for her work. She had every intention of taking the world by storm as the next Barbara Walters. Journalism was just in her blood. From the time that she was a small child, when company would come over, Corinne would pick up an ink pen or a comb or brush and interview each guest that came through the door. I recall one afternoon, a few members of the Highlands came over for a tea. Seven-year-old Corinne proceeded to interview all of the women there. I knew then that she was going to be a journalist. As the assistant editor, she was in charge of covering the major events that occurred on campus. There was nothing more pressing at the time, than the student protests related to race relations and the state of Black students at the University. Corrine was not heavily involved in the protests. In fact, she believed that those leading the charge were "noisemakers" who were looking for their 15 minutes of fame. The protests had gained local media attention and the leader, Essam Balu, stoked the fires of racial divide.

Corrine sat in the journalism department office reviewing stories submitted by non-staff students for possible inclusion in the next issue. She heard his signature walk, complete with the dragging of his right foot approaching the office.

"Ms. Ashworth, good to see you." Dr. Franklin said, speaking with a thick New England accent.

Dr. Franklin was the dean of the communications department and adviser for the student-led newspaper. He was also a bit creepy. His white skin looked ashen and his rounded back suggested that he was older than the 55 years he claimed to be. He wore the same brown polyester pants and beige tweed jacket every day. His thinning hair and flat paper-like nails beckoned for biotin.

"Doing well Dr. Franklin. What brings you here today?" She asked with trepidation. Dr. Franklin RARELY came to the journalism office. His role as the adviser was simply to make sure the students stayed out of trouble and didn't expose the university to liability.

"Well Miss Ashworth, we have some Black students that aren't happy about the university."

By this time, Dr. Franklin was leaning on the Xerox machine that was on the opposite end of the tiny office.

"The administration is trying to deal with the disruption in a dignified matter and we think that all these kids want is to be heard." He continued as Corrine looked on trying to figure out why he was talking to her about this.

"We think that you, being Black and all, could talk to the leader, Essam Bababalu, Blue, Bellyu. I don't know how to say those ethnic names. You know who he is; the dreadlock guy. We want you to interview him and figure out what he wants."

For one moment, Corrine considered saying no to his request. A coldness filled her gut. *Interviewing Robert...I mean Essam?* She felt immediately sick.

"Why me,?" she asked, already knowing the answer. Dr. Franklin walked over to her desk and knelt down.

"Corrine, you are a gifted journalist. You will make a fine

newscaster or writer to *Essence* or *Jet Magazine* one day. You Blacks know each other, and we think you can relate to him better than any of the other students on staff."

Corrine was keenly aware of the nature of the request. She was also aware that a story so big would garner her the front page and likely the attention of local media.

"I'll do it!" she said happily. "I'll reach out to Essam this afternoon and arrange the interview. Thank you for thinking of me Dr. Franklin."

Corrine didn't even take into consideration the bigoted undertones that Dr. Franklin spewed. Her focus was singular; get ahead by any means necessary. She didn't have a care or concern about the optics or the damage that would be done by her serving as the token Black reporter.

"Don't disappoint us, Corrine, we are counting on you." Dr. Franklin offered a salute and turned toward the door. "This interview could change your life…put you on the map Miss Ashworth." Corrine sat up in her chair and gave Dr. Franklin a wide smile.

Her excitement was emanating from every pore. *This is my chance! Now, all I have to do is talk to Essam…I mean…Robert.* The idea turned her stomach and a cold fear crept into her heart. She despised him and everything he stood for. Now, they were going to be face-to-face for the first time since that night freshman year.

16

We don't meet people by accident...

Corrine had been in school for just a few short months. Michigan was a good fit. Even the weather had agreed with her. The air was beginning to cool by November, and the leaves had long since turned various shades of orange, red, and gold. The campus glowed with color and anticipation for the Thanksgiving holiday. Helen had settled into life as a college student too. She and Corrine were more than roommates, they had become friends. Helen, as Corrine described her, was a very sensitive young woman who was often ignored by her parents. She was beginning to come into her own now that she was out of their house and was no longer forced to pretend to like them. Corrine had also made other friends with a few members of Epsilon Phi Upsilon, a sorority that was made up of the "it" girls on campus. The sorority was founded in 1910 specifically for Black collegiate women. To become a member of E Phi U was an honor bestowed on a select few. Corrine met the president of the chapter during freshman orientation, and she had taken particular interest in Corrine. Genelle Maxwell was from Prince George's County, Maryland. Corrine didn't know much about Genelle's family, and frankly, she didn't care. She knew that Genelle ran in the circles that Corrine wanted to be in, and because of that, their friendship was swift in the making. Midway through Corrine's freshman year, Genelle invited her to a soirée at the E Phi U sorority house. There, she would meet other members, as well and male students who were worthy of an invitation.

"Listen, we are very particular about the guest list, so don't bring a plus one, and definitely leave that roommate of yours at the dorm." Genelle's invitation came with restrictions and rules. "Also, you're not to wear anything sage or gray. These colors are reserved for members and you're not a member…yet. Understood?"

Corrine complied.

Getting ready for the soirée was nerve-racking. She pulled out every dress in her closet and tried on each one. Helen rated them, 0 to 10. The winner ended up being a black knee-length satin number with wide straps. She paired it with a red blazer and her black suede ankle boots. Helen sat on her bed waiting for Corrine to emerge from the bathroom. She walked out with a full face of subtle makeup, pearl earrings, and the agreed upon outfit.

"How do I look?"

Helen gave her a once over. "Fantastic! Knock 'em dead!"

Corrine grabbed her black leather purse and squealed with delight as she walked out of the door. She turned to address Helen.

"Thanks roomie…don't wait up!"

Arriving at the E Phi U house, Corrine thought, this was the beginning of the rest of her life. She imagined the atmosphere wouldn't match all of those college movies she had watched from the 1980s --a mix of stale beer and debauchery. The E house would be different. Walking up to the over sized wooden doors, she heard the faint sound of R&B music. *Teddy Riley? Really?* She'd imagined that E girls listened to classical or jazz, but certainly not ghetto music like New Jack Swing. Corrine had convinced herself that pop music was for the undignified and hip hop was for the criminal set. Though she loved the vibration of a solid baseline, she convinced herself that she was better than those hoodlums that rapped or moaned about sexing groupies. As she entered the foyer of the E Phi U house, she was shell-shocked. The E girls and their male guests looked like extras in a music video. The walls were literally sweating.

"Engine, engine number nine, on the New York transit line. If the train jumps off the tracks, pick it up, pick it up, PICK IT UP!"

Black Sheep pierced her ears and the whole crowd jumped up and down to the rhythm. Genelle spotted Corrine as she stood dumbfounded.

"Corrine...get in here! This is how us E girls party."

The other girls squealed out their signature call, *"Eeeeeeeee Phiiiiiii Ups!"* They all waved their right hands; index finger extended and made the letter E in the air. Genelle made her way to Corrine and grabbed her by the hand.

"I want you to meet someone."

Corrine stumbled through the crowd being towed by Genelle. They made their way to the kitchen. Corrine's eyes were down cast watching her footing to make sure she didn't trip and fall.

Finally, Genelle stopped and said, "Corrine Ashworth, Robert Livingston." Corrine's eyes shifted upward and there stood a guy with wide eyes and perfect teeth. Her mouth dropped.

Robert smiled brightly, "Well hello Miss Ashworth. Care to

dance?" Genelle released her hand and placed Corrine's gently in his, now outstretched. He was tall. Really tall. Robert, she surmised, was at least 6'3". His cocoa brown skin glistened with a hint of perspiration on his forehead. He wore a short haircut, complete with waves for days. He was dressed in Cross Colors jeans and a black tee-shirt that fit him perfectly. His tennis shoes looked like they were fresh out of the box, and he sported a thick, silver Patek Phillipe watch.

"Nice watch." Corrine said as Robert led her to the dance floor.

"Nice everything." He said as he winked at her and gently touched the small of her back. He swayed Corrine to the sound of "That's the Way Love Goes" by Janet Jackson.

Like a moth to a flame
Burned by the fire
My love is blind
Can't you see my desire?
That's the way love goes…

Corrine and Robert danced into the wee hours of the night. All the while, Genelle and the other E girls looked on to see just how close she was getting to Robert. The clock struck 2:00 AM and the lights that had been dimmed, shone brightly. Genelle stood on the top of the semi-circular stairway and raised her hand to hush the DJ.

"Thank you all for coming this evening. E girls need their beauty rest, so you don't have to go home, but you have to get outta here." With that, the members of the sorority let out a long squealing "Eeeeeeeeeee Phiiiiiiiiii Uppppppsssss." Robert released Corrine's hand to plug his ears.

"I will never get used to that sound," he said. Corrine thought, *I can't wait to be able to make that sound.* Robert offered to walk Corrine back to the dorm, and she happily accepted. As they approached the front door, Genelle and two other members of E Phi U stopped them in their tracks.

"Just where do you think you're going!" Genelle said as she pushed Robert in the chest.

"I was going to walk Corrine back to her dorm." He was nervous and Corrine didn't understand why Genelle and the others had made such a scene.

"Oh no you're not. She is going to stay here with us tonight. Say goodbye Corrine. We have things to discuss." The E girls stood with their arms crossed waiting for Robert to leave.

"Uh...well...I guess I'll see you on campus," Corrine said shamefacedly.

"Yeah...see ya." Robert turned and walked out the door. Corrine shut it behind him and quickly turned toward Genelle.

"What the heck was that about?"

"It was a test that you were about to fail. E girls aren't seen with random guys we just meet. If you haven't figured it out by now, Corrine, we are an exclusive group. The standards are very high, and we expect our members and prospective members to maintain a certain reputation. Dancing at a party is fine, but being seen with a guy walking you to your room causes speculation and would certainly disqualify you from membership."

Corrine nodded and understood their point, but Robert was F.I.N.E. Fine! And she wanted to get to know him better.

"I get it." Corrine said. "Who is this Robert Livingston anyway and why did you introduce us?" Corrine, Genelle, and the other girls sat on the fluffy gray sofa to chat.

"Well, Robert is an old family friend. We never dated, but he was definitely the hottest thing in PG County. His family owns a trucking company that will be passed down to him. His father is the president and CEO, and his mother is a socialite. Robert is smart, handsome, and a catch. I introduced him to you because you two have similar interests and his pedigree could boost yours…not that you don't come from a wonderful family. From what you have told me, it seems like your parents are very accomplished. Robert would be perfect for you to get where you want to go. Ya know what I mean?"

Corrine understood well. She wanted to be a member of the upper echelon of Black society, and this, she thought, was her ticket in. As a family, we were well off, but Robert's family was WELL OFF. Corrine had always had an affinity for the rich and popular and wanted to have that life as well.

Valentine's Day was a few weeks away and Corrine and Robert had been seeing each other every day since the soirée. Of course, they had maintained their dates in the public eye, given Genelle's prior admonishment, but it was getting harder and harder for the two to contain their feelings toward each other. They had snuck a kiss here and there when they thought no one was looking, but nothing more than that. After all, Corrine wanted to be an E girl, and E girls were virtuous, first. As she packed to come back home, Corrine's door was wide open. She and Helen had taken a break between studying for exams, to cleaning out their room.

What started as an organized space with the perfume of disinfectant wafting through the air and folded clothes, sharpened pencils, and empty trash cans, had been replaced with dusty floors, piles of dirty clothes in a corner, and unmade beds. College had taken a toll on their cleanliness and their commitment to keep their space livable. Their door was wide open as they hauled black bags full of trash and dirty clothes out the door and into the hallway. Corrine had her back turned as she was bent over a pile of clothes when a hand touched her behind.

"Hey!" She screamed. Flipping her hair out of her eyes, she raised her head to see Robert standing with his signature grin plastered on his perfect face.

"Oh…heyyyyyy." She purred.

"Hi. I see you're busy. I just wanted to see you. I am leaving in a few hours to get back to Maryland. Can you take a break?" Corrine didn't have the heart or the desire to say no.

"Sure, but I need to shower really quick." She reached for her shower caddy and Robert grabbed her hand.

"You can shower after. Let's go." *After what?* She thought.

Corrine and Robert traversed the campus next to each other, but not hand in hand. Robert had an agenda, but he didn't let Corrine in on it.

"Where are we going?"

Robert looked down and smiled, saying nothing. They ended up on the steps of his dorm.

"Ummm…where are we going?" Corrine asked, fully aware of where she was. She had never been in his room, but she knew where it was.

"I just gotta run up to grab a jacket. You can stay here. I'll be right back." He flipped his hand sarcastically, "I wouldn't want the E's to see you."

She giggled and said, "I'm a big girl. I go where I want to go." With that, the two boldly went through the door and made their way to his room. His room was immaculate. Corrine thought she had entered a different world. His walls were stark white and everything in his room was too. It was pure and clean and smelled like citrus.

"Wow. THIS is a room!" Corrine felt embarrassed with Robert having seen her room in such disarray. Her cheeks were flush, and she stood still, taking in the cloud-like space. It was peaceful and calm.

"Have a seat." Robert said. She scanned the room for a chair -- there wasn't one. She eyed his bed and he motioned to her to sit. Before she was firmly planted, Robert walked over and kissed Corrine passionately. She could hardly catch her breath. He pulled away and stared in her eyes. She slid further onto his bed, laid down and arched her back while pulling him toward her. Their bodies fit together like a hand in a glove. They tugged and pulled at each other's clothing in a haste to remove them. Corrine thought that she was going to explode. She had longed for Robert since she first saw him in the kitchen at the E house.

Their naked bodies were now damp with sweat and though they spoke no words, they communicated with every grind and moan. He was in her and they wound to an internal rhythm for what seemed like hours. Robert stroked her hair, and she wrapped her legs around his waist pulling him deeper and deeper inside of her. The rhythm sped up, and moments later, the rapid cadence ground to a halt filled with ecstasy. They breathed a sigh of relief and Robert, exhausted, kissed Corrine gently on her right shoulder. Corrine felt the warmth of his release on her right thigh and she smiled softly, then a sick feeling fell in her stomach. *Why am I feeling his cum on my thigh?* She thought. "Robert," she said, mouth dry and out of breath, "did the condom break.?"

"Condom?" He asked.

17

You didn't choose Hampton

Her journey to her full self started one day in Virginia. Nia didn't realize that her life was going to change, but the moment that we dropped her off at college years before, I knew that she was in the right place, and that our family was shifting again. We wouldn't know the gravity of the shift until years later.

Hampton University is a beautiful campus. It sits right against Hampton River and the scenery is breathtaking. Nestled along the banks of the Virginia Peninsula, near the mouth of the Chesapeake Bay, and founded in 1861, Hampton University began humbly with Mary Peake, a free Negro, teaching slaves, free Blacks, and Mulattos, even though the practice was forbidden by law. Under a simple oak tree, an institution and a legacy of highly educated people was born. Sam and I were elated that Nia had chosen an HBCU to attend. Though we would have been over the moon if she would have attended his alma mater, Lincoln or mine, Cheyney, we were glad that our influence to attend one of the over 100 HBCUs had made an impact. Corrine and James were not.

Flying into Virginia that August, was a harrowing experience. Traveling with family always is. Corinne, ever the planner, made sure that all of us had a designated bag which included our respective flight information, boarding pass, a bottle of water, and a snack to eat before we stepped on the plane. It was like we were on a third-grade field trip. I watched as Nia grew more and more agitated with her mother. Corrine doted on her, fluffed her hair, and kept reminding her of the responsibility as a Black woman in getting an education. Nia fell flat listening to her mother. She always wanted to go away to college, but she didn't want her mother's interference with her life. She had her own plan.

When we landed in Virginia Nia whispered to me, "Gram, it's almost over."

I didn't understand exactly what she meant, but I could only imagine that she was speaking about was her mother's controlling ways that smothered Nia for most of her life.

When Nia was in high school, Corinne made her join the French club, the fashion club, and run for ASB president. Though she lost the election, Nia was forced to be involved in activities that Corrine deemed "proper" for a girl of Nia's pedigree. She was the model student. Beautiful, smart, and well-liked by everyone, Nia was still miserable living under her mothers thumb. Corinne seemed to get pleasure watching her daughter become a member of the prestigious clubs and activities at Hilbrand High. She often commented that she wanted to see a paragraph of accomplishments under her name in Nia's yearbook picture.

"This is your last hurrah, girl!"

Ever defiant, Nia made sure that the yearbook stated only her name and the words "I'm out" under her picture. There was not one mention of clubs, activities, or even her GPA in that yearbook. I remember Corinne calling me enraged that her daughter had, once again, defied her and shamed the family name. She threatened to call the school board and demand a reprint of the yearbook before I was able to talk her down from taking such drastic, ridiculous measures.

Now, however, Nia was just moments away from being released from Corrine's tight, uncompromising grip. Walking into the dorm at Hampton, I was transported back to my own college days. The faint smell of mildew and humidity filled my nostrils. The energy that was pouring out of each dorm room was palpable. I watched as families hurried their children through and around each room holding bedspreads and trunks, boxes, and brooms. All the students looked awkwardly at one another, just waiting for their parents and grandparents to exit the dorms so that they could live their newfound lives. Corinne, with a tissue in hand, had assessed Nia's room before we reached her door. We walked in and saw Corrine wiping the windowsills in search of specks of dust. Her search must have been successful.

"Oh I'm not sure this room is going to work. The window faces West, there is dust everywhere, and that smell...It's making me ill. How on earth are you going to be able to get enough vitamin D with the window facing West?"

Nia and I looked at each other as Corinne continued surveying the room, the windows, and the dust.

"And this bed. There's no way you're going to get a good night's sleep on this bed." Corrine said with disgust.

"I'm going to have to talk to the housing director about these accommodations. These simply will not do. I knew we should have gone to Michigan."

Corinne had always believed that HBCUs were inferior to her all-white education. She had selected Michigan as her school of choice, and never batted an eye. She knew the caliber of student that HBCUs produce because her father, and I, were both proud graduates of a historically Black college. For some reason, however, Corinne believed that her white education was superior to the one that Nia's was about to embark upon as a student. As she floated out of the room talking to herself about *Posturepedic* beds and West facing windows, we began to unpack Nia's things. A lamp here, a bedspread there, and of course her favorite teddy bear.

"I cannot believe you brought this thing to college," I said.

We were finishing the tedious task of putting Nia's clothes in the small closet, when Corinne bounded back into the room, "We're leaving. This school, this room, and these people are not what I had in mind for you Nia. I agreed to the Black college thing because of your grandparents, but we have choices now. We can go to any school we want to attend. This is nice for some, but not for you." She began gathering boxes.

"What?" Nia said. "Mom, I'm not going anywhere. I picked this school, and I am staying. It's my dream school and I'm done with you choosing what I do! Enough, mom. I'm staying." Nia was seething with anger.

Sam and I stood quietly as James dutifully wipe down the desk and began plugging in Nia's laptop and television.

"Listen, I accepted the fact that you wanted to go to this kind of school. But I will not have my daughter living in squalor." Corinne said.

Nia stepped forward, as close to her mother as humanly

possible, and said, "Mom I'm staying. If you don't like it here, you can leave." I stepped forward next to my granddaughter.

"Nia, you know Gram loves you. But you're out of line, watch your tone and your words."

Corrine wasn't a fighter. In fact, she hated any kind of conflict. She lived blissfully unaware of all the things that swirled around her life, her family, her marriage, and her child. Her eyes were covered with rose colored glasses, and everything had to look perfect. I knew, deep down, that nothing was perfect. Corinne looked at me, grabbed her purse, and stormed out of the room. That was the last time she ever entered Nia's dorm room at Hampton.

I looked at James and Sam and we played a game of mental Rochambeau. *Who was going to be the one to follow Corinne out of the room and check on her to see what we could do to squash the tension between she and her daughter?* I was duly elected, by the look in both of their eyes. I found myself walking down the oatmeal-colored hallway. The smell of disinfectant and new college joy was permeating the air. The coldness of the cinder block walls, that were heavily painted, were a runway for me as I walked slowly toward my now weeping daughter. She looked so small in that hallway. Corinne had learned how to be a bright light. Her job required it. But in that moment, she was small, meek, dim. Corrine appeared almost childlike. Her feelings were hurt, but instead of talking through issues, she took her ball and went home. I couldn't imagine what triggered her enough to storm out of her daughter's room on the first day that her only child entered college. Perhaps it was because she was losing her daughter and her nest was now empty. Perhaps it was because something darker and more painful was inside of her heart.

I found Corinne in a corner at the very end of the hallway. She was uncharacteristically sad and inconsolable. Tears streamed down her cheeks like a river, as I approached her.

"Mama, why does she hate me so much?" Corrine asked.

I lifted her chin with my hand, and said, "She doesn't hate you, Corinne. She's just not you."

She looked deep in my eyes and stared at me as though it was the first time that she had heard that. For so many years Corinne and Nia had a tense relationship. Surely, she knew that her daughter was different than she was. She hoped against hope that Nia would be what she wanted her to be, but she wasn't. I didn't quite understand the depth or breadth of Corinne's sadness, after all Nia was a good girl. She was beautiful and accomplished, and here we were dropping her off at college, and even that wasn't enough for Corinne. In her own subtle way, I believe she understood what I was saying, but couldn't accept the truth. Nia and Corrine were two different people -- one coming from the other, but so different. In fact, they reminded me of Corinne and myself. I had done a wonderful job of hiding my true being for so long. I was a wife, and a mother, then a woman. I had lived my life in those roles so protected and controlled, that Corinne knew would never be able to see me in any other way. I hoped secretly, in my heart, that I could be more like my granddaughter, but time, age, and life would not allow for it.

"Let her be, Corinne. If what you've done to raise her is right, she will land on her feet. She may not land on the street that you paved for her, but she will land on her feet." I said.

Corrine brushed the tears from her eyes, and seemed to come

back to her controlled, rehearsed self.

"Well, we'll see."

With that, Corinne slung her Prada handbag onto her shoulder, straightened her blouse, tossed her hair, and walked down the steps to the lobby of the dorm. I stood in the hallway, dumbfounded. She left. She didn't enter that room ever again. She left her daughter waiting, wondering, wishing for her mother to just accept her for who she was. I gathered myself, inhaled a deep cleansing breath, looked to heaven, and began the long, lonely walk back down the oatmeal-colored hall. I entered Nia's room with six watchful eyes waiting to hear what happened between Corinne and I. I did my level best to feign a smile, I said, "Your mother is having a very difficult time letting you go sweetheart. Give her time." I lied. Corinne wasn't having a hard time at all, at least, for the reason I said. Corrine, herself, was holding onto a secret. I knew it, but she didn't know that I did. I was waiting for the right time to bring her out of the shadows of her own life and seek shelter in the sun. Lord knows I know what it feels like to hold secrets.

Nia could hardly wait for us to get out of her room. I could feel her wanting us to go so that she could live her life and experience college in the way that she wanted. In the distance, I could hear music and the faint tap and chant of a fraternity showing off their latest step routine. It was electrifying. I was transported back to my own time at Cheyney. Corinne was still sitting in the lobby refusing to go back up to the room after all of the unpacking and cleaning had been done. James and Sam said their goodbyes to Nia. As they left her now pink and yellow room, where sheer curtains dressed the windows and posters of Prince and *Starry Night* adorned the walls, I watched as she sat crossed legged on the pink bedspread that was draped over her twin bed. We had doused it with throw pillows, and a soft sheepskin rug would caress her feet when she uncrossed her legs to stand. Her desk was outfitted with a lamp, her computer, books, school supplies, and a framed photograph of she and I. I stood in the middle of the room watching her unfold and open up to this new life.

"Gram, I'm here." Nia said. She looked around the room with awe and wonder in her eyes.

"Yes you are sweetheart. I want you to take this opportunity to learn and to grow into a bold being," I said trying to hold back tears. "This reminds me of my time in college. Savor every moment and learn as much as you can inside and outside of the classroom."

I was beginning to feel the emotional gravity of the moment. I had watched her take her first step, my only grandchild. And now, she was going to be miles away taking another step without me or her parents there to hold her hand. Nia's eyes fell softly on my face "I will Gram," she said softly.

"Don't you worry at all about your mother. She's wounded, and I think this is just all too much for her to take. I'll talk to her, but in the meantime, you have yourself a ball here at Hampton. These are the best days of your life."

I smiled brightly and Nia looked at me with her eyebrow raised, "Gram, my best days are just beginning. I know this is gonna be a great experience, but I have a whole life to live, and I can't wait to see what happens next."

I stood there thinking about what Nia said. Was she right? Were our best days always in front of us, or were they behind us? Either way, in her 18 years of life, she had garnered so much wisdom. I didn't even know how to process what she said. All I could think about, was that my granddaughter, was now going to be 1,500 miles away from me, living her best life.

I checked my watch and saw that the hour was 4:16 PM. It was time for us to go. I reached down and embraced Nia as tightly as I could and whispered in her ear, "I love you sweetheart study hard and have a ton of fun." Nia didn't speak at all she just held me a bit tighter. As we released our embrace, I walked away knowing that my granddaughter was going to be OK.

I got to the lobby of the dorm and saw Sam, James, and Corrine waiting for me there. Corinne stared at me waiting for assurance that Nia was OK. I assured her. I reached my arms out to Corrine, "She's going to be just fine. You and James have done a wonderful job in raising her. I can't wait to see what happens next." Corinne offered a half smile, squeezed my hands, and walked toward the front door.

18

Everything and nothing changed

That night, as we headed back to Hilbrand from the airport, the car was quiet. None of us spoke a word. I imagined that Nia was at a block party, had made friends with her dorm mates, and was dancing the night away. I thought about her walking through the yard, checking out all of the young, educated, men that lined the walkways assessing the new women on campus. The sheer joy of knowing that your life is just beginning must be exhilarating for young people. At my age, there was nothing new.

James and Corinne dropped me and Sam off at home, and we walked into the door of our house. Everything was as we left it. I could play in my mind exactly how the evening would progress. Sam would take his shoes off at the door, he, in his white socks, would shuffle across the hardwood where he would ease into his brown whiskey leather chair. He would lean back and recline. Then, he would beckon, "Doris? Gorgeous? Can you get me a beer?" I will have already been at the refrigerator popping a top.

Our life was predictable. I would walk in with an ice-cold Budweiser in my right hand, and bag of pork rinds in my left. By this time, Sam would be reared back in his chair with the remote control in his hand. He would flip from CNN, to Fox News, back to CNN. All while shaking his head saying, "What's the world coming to?" I would sit bored on the corner of the couch, unresponsive. He wasn't asking the question for a response, but rather just to hear himself speak. My activity would be to sit on the couch for about 5 minutes, and then find some menial tasks to perform around the house. Wiping off the counter tops in the kitchen. Making sure there were toilet paper rolls in the guest bathroom. Puttering around the house looking for something to do. Eventually, Sam would fall asleep in that easy chair, and I would have to awaken him with a shake on the shoulder. He would act startled as though this scene didn't play out every single day of our lives. I would hop in the shower, moisturize my body with coconut oil, climb into bed, and fall fast asleep before Sam even reached the covers. That was our cadence every night.

I would awaken in the morning and make him cottage cheese with pineapple and scrambled eggs, with a dash of Tabasco sauce. Our days were rarely spontaneous. Sam may go to the hardware store to buy screws or a power tool. I, to the Senior Community Center to volunteer reading to children. Every day was the same. Our life was predictable. There was never any excitement or passion. I suppose that's because Sam had so much turmoil in his own life as a young man, he wanted routine now in his golden years. After so many years of marriage, I didn't know any different, I didn't know if I wanted any different. So, there we sat in our lives doing the same things every day for decades.

A few weeks after we arrived back from Virginia, Nia called me. She was talking a mile a minute about all of the wonderful things that happened in just a few short weeks that she had been at Hampton. She had started her classes and loved every one of her professors.

She talked about the energy on a Black college campus.

"Gram, there is so much to do here! My English professor wrote the textbook that he is teaching from. He wrote the book! Last week, Nikki Giovanni came to campus on a whim just to sit in on the class and talk about her poetry. It's crazy! Nikki Giovanni! Not to mention, the fine men!" she said. "Not only are they fine, but they're smart too!"

We giggled like schoolgirls when she spoke of all of the wonderful things that were happening.

"That's Black college life." I said.

She had established her own tribe of girls. They were from all over the country, but they bonded over the fact that they all had issues with their mothers. I told her that she should start a club. She laughed at the idea. She mentioned that her classes were difficult, but her professors made them so exciting.

"Gram it's like I want to learn everything they know."

I couldn't believe how excited she was, but I knew that feeling. When I walked onto the campus of Cheyney University, I felt like I had been reborn. It was energizing being on that campus. So many things were going on and so many people from all different walks of life lived amongst one another, learning, growing, and exploring. Never in my wildest dreams would I have thought that I would be on a campus learning about history and myself, mathematics, biology, chemistry, all taught by Black people. It was the very best time of my life, and Nia, was now experiencing the exact same thing. She mentioned that there was a particular group of girls who befriended her.

"They're sorority girls Gram. We hang out together on occasion and they've mentioned that I would be just the right fit for their group. Can you believe it? Me, an E girl?" We giggled together, but I reminded Nia that being a member of an auspicious organization was a privilege. That's something she may want to consider, after she masters her studies. She agreed, and we said our goodbyes.

"Gram, I miss you." Nia said.

"I miss you too sweetheart, I'll see you at Thanksgiving. And fear not, I will be making sweet potato pies this year." We hung up the phone after our mutual I love you's and I sat in my family room and grinned. My granddaughter was basking in the brightness of the sun.

That evening, James, Sam, Corrine, and I had dinner together. We went to James and Corinne's house at her invitation. She was an exceptional cook and enjoyed sharing new recipes and flavors with us. With Nia now gone, we had so much time to spend with one another. I thought that it would be a good opportunity for me and Corinne to get to know each other better as women, not just mother and daughter. I soon discovered that Corrine had no interest in establishing that type of relationship.

"Mama, can you believe what's been going on in the Highlands?" Corrine squealed.

The Highlands were a women's organization that Corinne and I were members of. I was an alumni member who had paid her dues in service for over 30 years. I did not have much involvement with the day-to-day operations of the organization, and I certainly didn't have time for the latest gossip. I had joined because Sam wanted us to be part of "the right circles" back in the 1970s. Corrine had taken a more active role in her membership. She was now the vice president, and the resident gossip of the group. She had something to say about everyone in the organization, which was interesting because the tenets were all about uplifting Black women and the community.

"I was horrified to learn that Ursula's youngest son had decided to leave college to go 'find himself,' What does that even mean?" Corinne said with disgust in her voice. "These children have no idea the sacrifices that were made for them. And their reluctance to do as they've been instructed is just beyond what I can ever imagine. I know Nia has been a lot of things, but at least she's in school, and at least she's majoring in law so that she could actually become something in this world."

I listened as Corrine went on and on about her hopes and dreams for Nia. I knew better than to entertain the discussion by offering a retort. I knew that Nia was going to dance to the beat of her own drum, and she had no interest in doing what Corinne wanted her to do. There was a certain level of defiance that this generation has toward their parents. They want to do their own life, in their own way, on their own terms. I never supported Nia exhibiting any disrespect toward her parents, but Sam and I both agreed that Nia was her own person and had always been her own person. What we didn't understand was why Corinne was so hell bent on her fitting into the mold, the box that she had created for herself, Nia, and James.

"Enough Corrine." James said sternly. "Your parents did not come over here to listen to you gossip about those hens. Let's just eat and have a wonderful conversation about something other than the Highlands."

I was grateful for his interjection. The last thing I wanted to do was talk about those women. Corinne huffed as she scooped potatoes onto the plates. Everything looked delicious. Corrine was proud of the tablescape that she had created, and I complimented her on the aroma of the food. Everything matched. Tablecloths too. The fresh flowers were arranged in small clear vases lining the center of the table. Corinne had learned how to be a gracious and wonderful hostess. She retreated to the kitchen for a moment, only to emerge with a silver platter full of roast beef. The smell of pepper and rosemary permeated the air.

"Awww shucks. Imma eat good tonight daughter." Sam said while rubbing his bulbous stomach.

She prepared grilled baby asparagus, wrapped in bacon, drizzled with a small touch of balsamic vinegar and olive oil. Everything looked, smelled, and tasted amazing. After dinner, James and Sam retreated to the family room to watch the sports highlights while Corrine and I tended to the kitchen.

"So, have you talked to Nia lately?" Corrine asked as she scrubbed the pots and pans. "As a matter of fact, I spoke to her earlier today." I said. "She's doing well. When's the last time you talked to her?"

"When we dropped her off."

I stopped in my tracks. I had been wiping the kitchen counter and I turned to look at Corrine.

"You haven't spoken to your daughter at all?" I asked.

Corrine stopped scrubbing, "I'm not sure I want to talk to her, and I know that she doesn't want to talk to me."

Corrine said. I couldn't imagine not speaking to my child. Corrine was a tough nut to crack, but she was still my daughter. I didn't know the details or why their relationship was so volatile, but I had my suspicions. I mustered up as much strength as I could, dried my hands and grabbed the shoulders of my daughter, who was still standing aloof at the sink.

"Corrine? What is it? Why are you so hard on that child? She has never given you an ounce of trouble." I asked.

Corrine didn't say a word. Her head dropped, and I began to hear her whimper softly. I lifted her head, and for the first time since we left the dorm, I consoled my daughter who looked like a wounded child in need of a mother's love. Her head slumped down again.

"I don't know what's wrong with me Momma. I just can't find joy."

I didn't have an answer for her because I didn't know what she was talking about. She had everything. She lived with a wonderful husband, had a beautiful daughter, a thriving career in journalism, and a lovely home. She had every reason to have joy in her life, so I thought. I put my arms around her and hugged her as tightly as I could. I envisioned that I could squeeze out whatever was hurting. But I knew that it wouldn't. Her wounds were too deep, and she had buried them for so long that they were beginning to consume her.

"It's going to be OK daughter." I said, but I wasn't even sure that was true.

19

Anemic

Corrine flew home a few weeks after her encounter with Robert. She had been offered a semester long internship that would be a substitute for her advanced English course that she was enrolled in. She had applied months before the soirée, and she been accepted a few days before...**THAT** day. She panicked as she thought about the unprotected sex that she had with Robert. No condom, no birth control, with AIDS running rampant and cure-less. She was a nervous wreck. Her "first time" had been careless and dangerous.

She had been a relatively "good girl" her whole life and never intended to be loose. Me and her father had raised her to remain a virgin until marriage. I struggled to continue the "virtue lie" that I imposed on her when I, myself, had Rome in my past. She arrived to the house in a taxi.

"Mommmmmmmm...I'm hommmmeeeee." I rushed from the bedroom, beating Sam to the door.

"My baby! Oh let me look at you." I hugged Corrine tighter than I had ever hugged her before. Sam separated us, "Let me get a look at my baby girl!" The smell of roasted chicken filled the room as Corrine placed her bag down in the hallway leading to her room.

"You look wonderful...a little thin, but wonderful." I said.

Corrine smiled, "Thanks Mom. Dorm food is not HOME food."

"Well, I made your favorites." I proudly guided her into the kitchen where I had prepared a feast of roasted chicken, Caesar salad, red potatoes, green beans, and sweet potato pie.

"Mom! It looks like you are feeding an army!"

"Not an army, love, just a starving college student." We laughed together and I fixed her a plate.

It was great to have Corrine home that summer. The well-paid internship was hard work, but she was working in the field that she loved. She came home exhausted every day. The job wore her out, even though she loved it. She barely spoke, and her eating was spotty, at best. I suggested that she see her primary doctor while she was at home. I knew that she had had a history of asthma as a child and anemia as a teen. I walked into Corrine's room. It was dark and she was laying on the bed, face down, asleep. I touched her forehead to check for a fever. There was none. I writhed my hands debating on whether I should wake her for dinner or leave her be. I decided to just watch her sleep. She stayed perfectly still as she lay.

When she was a small child, I would often check her when she slept. Her asthma was severe, and her breathing was often labored to the point that I thought she had stopped all together. She had grown out of the severe asthma attacks, which required visits to the ER and my constant monitoring. I was transported right back to those days. Old habits die hard. I stood in her room for about 30 minutes before Sam called me from the family room. I snapped out of my daydream thinking about Corrine as a child.

"Is she OK?" He asked.

"Yes. She's fine. I think she is just catching up on her sleep. She's breathing normally." I said.

The next morning, Corrine made an appointment to see our family doctor, Dr. Phillip Betts. Dr. Betts and his wife Yolanda had been friends of ours for years. Phillip and Sam met in the military, and we all reconnected, years later, when we found out that they had moved to Hilbrand. Dr. Betts had taken care of everyone in our family.

"Mom, I'm going to see Dr. Betts at 10:00 AM. But, I'm gonna go past the Coffee Haus for a coffee first."

"Do you need me to go with you?" I asked. I was hoping that she would say yes, but I knew she wouldn't.

"No. I think I can handle it." Corrine was independent and she didn't need me fretting over her. I was worried and she knew it. Her calmness calmed me.

"OK. Well, just let me know..."

The details of what happened after she arrived at Dr. Betts' office were relayed to me years later. She told me that when she walked into his office, his nurse did the standard tests; blood pressure, temperature, height, weight.

"You've lost some weight since your last visit. Are you eating enough at school?"

"I think so." Corrine said.

"Well, you may want to add a little more protein in your diet. I'll make a note on your chart. Go on into room 8 and Dr. Betts will be right in." Dr. Betts was a short, slight Black man with a thick Jamaican accent. He knocked on the door and opened it.

"Well, there. Hellooo my Corrine. College student

extraordinaire." Dr. Betts had a sunny disposition he was always happy.

"Hi doc." Corrine's eyes drifted from his face and rested on the gray wall behind him.

"So, child, what brings you in?"

"I haven't felt good lately. I'm tired. I think the anemia is back." Corrine fancied herself an expert in diagnosing her own ailments.

"Maybe I just need more iron pills."

Dr. Betts chimed in, "You're going to med school, huh?" He said with a sarcastic tone. "When was the first day of your last period?" Corrine was about to answer, but she stopped herself. *I haven't had a period since I got home.*

"Huh?"

"First day of your last period?" Dr. Betts repeated. His smile turned into a look of concern. "I don't know." Corrine said.

Her mind began racing. *OK, I was on my period during study session for history*

class because I asked Tyra for a tampon. When was that? Oh God. When was that?

Corrine was racking her brain for answers.

"OK, let's get some blood work and see what's going on. Changes in your cycle are normal when you make drastic changes in your life. Let's see what's going on hormonally and make sure the anemia isn't causing any issues. I'll have the nurse come in and draw some blood." Dr. Betts noted Corrine's chart and walked out of the room.

The nurse returned to the room with a series of vials and a syringe with a long plastic tube attached on a silver tray.

"OK Corrine, squeeze this and let's fill these vials up and get them to the lab." She watched as the warm red blood slowly filled the tubes. She started to feel a bit queasy as it drained from her veins, but she swallowed hard and regained her composure.

"OK. All done." The nurse said confidentially. "I'm going to have the lab tech run some quick tests and Dr. Betts will be back in a second. In the meantime, doctor wants you to do a urinalysis." She handed Corrine a plastic cup that had a blue screw top. It was sealed and it bore her name, birth date, and the date of collection scribbled in ink. Corrine took the cup and made her way to the bathroom that was down the hall from room 8. Filling the cup was an exercise in acrobatics. As she filled the reservoir with her pale-yellow urine, she prayed, *Dear God, please don't let me be...* She couldn't even say the word.

I waited nervously for Corrine to call me. It was 12:37 PM when the phone rang.

"Hello?"

"Hey mom. I'm just about to leave Dr. Betts' office. He said my anemia is back. I'm gonna go to the pharmacy to get my iron pills. See, I told you I was fine."

"Oh that's good news. OK. I'll be home when you get here. Love you."

"Love you too." I was relieved. There's nothing worse than not knowing what's wrong with your child. My gut told me that something was wrong, and I was glad that it was only anemia, which meant that all she needed was an increase in iron supplements. It was welcomed news. I told Sam and waited for Corrine to come home.

20

What Happens in the Dark Always Comes to Light

I was grateful that it was just Corrine's anemia. She had such difficulty in her youth with the asthma and then, as a teen with anemia. She needed to take better care of herself. I was determined to get her back on track, and I had a month to do it before she returned to Michigan. She walked in the house with a smile on her face.

"Anemia." I said.

"Yep. Gotta take vitamins and start eating better. Dr. Betts said that I was pretty healthy, but I need to pay more attention to my diet and get more sleep."

Corrine had made her way to the kitchen and was washing an apple. She took a large bite,

"He also said that the vitamins might make me a little queasy and that it was normal." I stared at her as she moved quickly throughout the house. It felt like she was walking off nervous energy, but I chalked it up to her just being excited.

"OK, Mom. I'm gonna go change and get outta here. I'm meeting some friends for dinner. Love you."

"How late will you be out? Me and Dad want to spend a little time with you. You'll be back at school in a month."

"Not a month, 23 days. I'm leaving in 23 days. I don't know what time I'll be home. I have plenty of quarters, so I'll call you and let you know."

"OK. But what about dinner? Daddy and I haven't had you to ourselves since you got home."

"I know mom," she said while rolling her eyes, seeming annoyed. "We can have dinner this weekend, OK?" She didn't wait for a response. Before I knew it, she had walked swiftly to her room, and I heard the door close.

When Corrine got to her room, she began pacing the floor. Her nervous energy had turned into pure panic. She had tried to compose herself in my presence and she wondered if her act was convincing enough to throw me off the scent of what was brewing in her soul. *How could she have let this happen?* The flood gates of her grief and fear overtook her. She cried into her pillow, trying to keep her secret shame undetectable to anyone that would pass by her room. She wiped the tears that were fast flowing from her eyes, and hoped that she had fooled me. For awhile, she did. Dr. Betts had assured her that he wouldn't tell Sam and I what was **REALLY** wrong with her.

Corrine was pregnant. She paced the floor trying to devise a plan to leave Hilbrand before she started showing. Twenty-three days would put her right at 3 months. She didn't have the foggiest idea when a woman began to show, but she couldn't bear being in Hilbrand with the evidence of her indiscretion growing in her belly. She thought that she could hide it better at school. She plotted how the Fall weather would help her hide her bulging belly because she could wear over sized clothing and coats. Mid-pace, she stopped and stared at herself in the full-length mirror. *It had only been one time. One time with Robert. There was no one else.*

Her mind was racing, and she spoke to herself again this time, in a whisper, "What am I going to tell him? Am I going to tell him?" She began pacing again, "I have two more years of college. How am I going to take care of a baby?" So many things were running through her mind, she didn't hear me calling her to the phone.

"Cooorrrriinnnnnneeeee…telephone. It's Dr. Betts." Corrine gathered herself, opened the door to her room and walked to the corded phone that was housed on the kitchen wall. She glanced at me as she walked by.

"Hello Dr. Betts." On the other line, Dr. Betts inquired about how she was feeling.

"Oh, I feel fine." He told her that he had gotten the results of the blood test and it showed that, she was indeed pregnant and about 6 weeks along.

"OK. Dr. Betts she said. Anemia. Iron. Right." Dr. Betts told her that she needed talk to us as soon as possible.

"Corrine?" He said, his heavy accent piercing through the phone, "You need to tell them. This is very serious, especially for a young woman, like yourself."

Corrine ignored his admonishment. "Yes, 2 pills a day. Got it."

Dr. Betts replied, "I see that you aren't interested in speaking to them. I understand. I don't agree, but I understand." He was disappointed. "At least make an appointment with an OB/GYN in Michigan as soon as possible since pre-natal care is essential to ensure the health of yourself and the baby."

"I'll do that as soon as I get back to Michigan. Don't you worry.

Well…thank you for your call, Dr. Betts. Give the family my best. Goodbye."

They hung up and Corrine composed herself again. She had no intention of ever telling Sam and I about the pregnancy. She kept it a secret from everyone, for decades.

Arriving back in Michigan 23 days after her diagnosis caused Corrine even more stress. She told no one about her condition, not even Helen. When Helen made her way into their room, now in an upper-classmen dorm, she immediately wrapped Corrine in a tight hug.

"Damn, girl! Your mom must have been cooking the whole summer. You put on a few." Helen giggled and started poking at Corrine's swelling belly. Avoiding the touch, Corrine scooted away, shielding her secret and trying to muster up a smile.

"Yep. Mom's cooking filled me up and out." The two traded stories about what they had done in the Summer. Helen had spent it traveling the world. She didn't even go home to see her parents.

"Why would I go see them when I could spend my summer eating pasta in Italy and frolicking in the South of France on my parent's dime?"

Corrine lied about her summer adventures. Truthfully, after she found out about the baby, she spent her days and nights mapping out plan for the rest of her life. She had considered abortion, but she didn't have the heart to do it. She thought about raising the baby by herself and finishing college with an child on her hip. Nothing made sense. She was a child herself.

"Yeah so I spent my summer with family and friends all day. I had a blast. I traveled a little, but I stayed close to home most of the time." Corrine said.

"I would have stayed home too if my momma cooked like your momma!" Helen said with a hint of sarcasm in her voice.

Corrine was listening and engaging with her roommate, but her mind was a million miles away. She needed to tell Robert. This baby, after all, was his too.

"Hey, I'm going to the café. I'll be back." Corrine dashed out to look for Robert. The campus wasn't quite full yet, but it was already buzzing with excitement. It was still hot and muggy outside and Corrine, was sweaty and hotter than usual. She scanned the campus for any sign of Robert. Deep in thought and laser focused, she searched for him. In her sight line, she saw Genelle.

"Hey girl!" Genelle said. "How was your summer?" "Good. Yours?"

"Amazing," she said. "My parents rented a yacht and we stayed out for an entire month. It was just what I needed."

Genelle gave Corrine a once over, "You look great. You put a little meat on those bones. Robert may have to fight some guys this year!"

Corrine giggled nervously.

"And speaking of this year, we are going to have a new line in December. You should start getting ready."

Genelle winked. *Oh shit. E Phi U was this year. Oh my God,* Corrine thought.

"Hey have you seen Robert anywhere?" Corrine had ignored Genelle's topic of discussion. Not on purpose, but because she had a more pressing issue to discuss.

Genelle, furled her eyebrows and stood perplexed by Corrine's lack of enthusiasm, "Yeah. I saw him by the English building. Be warned, though, he's a little different than what you remember. Anywho, gotta go. I'll see you around."

Genelle reached into her Louis Vuitton clutch, pulled out a pair of Chanel sunglasses and bid Corrine farewell. Corrine didn't even respond to the hasty goodbye. She was on a mission.

She made her way to the English building. As she approached it, she saw that a small crowd of Black students were gathered around one guy who seemed to have them all mesmerized. They held signs that read, *Fair Treatment* and *No Justice, No Peace*, and *Our Black is Beautiful*. Corrine wondered what in the world, the students could possibly be protesting. The ringleader stood in the center of the crowd.

"We must take our rightful place and position on this campus. They have no problem with us being on the field or the court, but there are fewer than 10 Black professors here. We need to lead in the classroom and in the boardroom!"

The crowd erupted with cheers.

"Our money pays their salary. Our demands must be honored!"

Corrine squinted to see if she could locate Robert in the sea of discontent. The guy in the middle had a bullhorn and was spewing propaganda and using buzz phrases to rally the crowd. Corrine looked at him and a strange feeling came over her. This guy looked like Robert, sounded like Robert, but it wasn't Robert. Robert was clean cut and wore a Patek Phillipe watch. This guy was wearing some African smock, had twists in his hair, and layers of string bracelets on his wrists. Robert would never be seen in this melee. She caught his eye and he smiled. *Holy shit. It was Robert!*

He maneuvered through the crowd and eventually stood nose-to-nose with Corrine.

"Robert? What did you do to yourself?" Corrine asked as the crowd dispersed. Robert had ended the protest early. Seeing Corrine stirred up other feelings that he wanted to address and they didn't have anything to do with equality on campus. He had missed Corrine all summer and she thought that he couldn't wait to pick up where they had left off.

"Damn girl, it's good to see you too. And my name isn't Robert anymore. I legally changed it over the summer. I am now Essam. Essam Balu."

Corrine looked confused, "What? Wait? What?"

"Yes. It means *safeguard*."

Over the Summer, Robert, Essam had volunteered in A Muslim village in Uganda, building homes for the poor. While he was there, he began interacting with the townspeople and other religious leaders to discover his true roots. He told Corrine that he was done with the Western way of living and was taking a more holistic and socially conscious approach to life.

"Wait? What?" Corrine responded. She listened as he talked about his experiences, the Ugandan culture, his conversion to Islam, and the ways that it changed his life. He had even decided to be celibate.

"The fruit of a woman should be honored and savored. I have committed to not taste again until I am married." *Too little, too late.* Corrine thought. "I am on a quest to free my people, our people from the Eurocentric norms and instead, embrace their own roots."

Corrine sat staring at the man that she laid with just a few months prior, and she didn't recognize him. How was she supposed to tell him that he was going to be a father? She didn't. She looked into his eyes and saw the hope for his future vanishing if he knew he was having a baby. A child would dash his dreams and it didn't make sense for both of them to lose what they were working so hard to achieve. She listened more, and when Essam was finished and finally got around to ask her about her summer.

"What did you do over the Summer, Corrine?"

"Nothing. It was uneventful."

The man, who had wooed her at the soirée, made her toes curl in his room, and was the father of a child he would never know about, was not who stood before her. Everything had changed, and Robert had no idea how much.

Days turned into weeks, weeks turned into months and her belly was growing rapidly. She had managed to get to the mall and buy 2 dozen over-sized flannel shirts. They were semi-stylish, warm, and provided the perfect coverage for her belly. On several occasions, she had to fake menstrual cramps, and wrap up clean menstrual pads to make sure Helen didn't get wind of her secret. She showered late at night or early in the morning to avoid being found out. The morning sickness that she experienced was explained away with the fake iron pills. She was taking pre-natal vitamins daily and her trips to the OB/GYN were in secret too. She would tell Helen and Genelle that she was working on a confidential news story or conducting an interview for an upcoming exposé. That way, she could leave campus, go to her doctor's appointments, and no one questioned her.

For months, she had thrown everyone, including me and her father off the scent. She rarely called home, but we chalked that up to her being busy with school, friends, and her initiation to Epsilon Phi Upsilon.

"So, how is the pledge thing going?" I asked. When Corrine first got wind of the sororities interest in her becoming a member, she could barely contain her excitement. "Are you going to the interest meeting that Genelle mentioned?"

"Uhhh…I don't think so." Corrine said.

"Really? What happened? Do you need a dress? I can pick something up and mail it to you. I know there are color restrictions. What do you think about pink? You've always looked pretty in pink." Her affect was flat. It seemed strange, but I let it go.

No, I don't need a dress. I need a tent to cover this pregnant belly of mine.

"No, mom. I have a dress. I'm thinking of waiting until next year. Just have a lot on my plate this year and…."

Corrine didn't sound convinced that her decision was the right one, and I knew that there had to be more to the story. I kept my hunch to myself. I listened as she offered excuse after excuse. It didn't make sense, but I knew my daughter well enough to know that whatever was going on, she would handle it.

"If that's what you want dear…" A mother knows their child, and I knew mine. Something wasn't right. I didn't know what it was and wouldn't find out the truth for years. When I did, everything about Corrine, Nia, and their relationship made sense.

Thanksgiving was just around the corner and Corrine knew that if she came home, her secret would be out. She couldn't go home with Essam either. She and Essam hadn't spoken since the protest and, although he would send love notes with African proverbs on them, he wasn't her type anymore. He had become too earthy for her taste and their love affair fizzle into mist. Helen offered to have Corrine as a guest, but Corrine declined.

"No offense, roomie, but your family seems a little scary!" Helen laughed in agreement.

When I called to inquire about her Thanksgiving plans, she told me that she was working on a project. She said that she needed to be in the community without the safety and security of campus. I understood her perspective, but I missed my girl. Sam and I would have a nice Thanksgiving for two.

The Friday after Corrine feasted on a meal of Lay's potato chips and a Snapple, her stomach began to cramp. The pain lasted the better part of the night and into the wee hours of morning. She battled the pain writhing on the floor of her dorm, alone. At about 4:00 AM, the pain had become unbearable, and she made her way to the elevator using the cinder block walls as a means of support. When she could no longer walk, she crawled. The dorm was empty and there was no one there to help her. She made her way through the foyer, and into the parking lot where her car was. By the time she sat in the seat, her water broke. *Oh my God. I am about to have a baby.*

Corrine drove herself the 3 miles to the hospital. Terrified and feeling faint, she managed to park in the *Ambulance Only* spot right in front of the Emergency Room door. An orderly was walking through the automatic sliding doors when she cried out in pain. He heard her scream and immediately summoned doctors and nurses to come to Corrine's aid. By the time the team raised her weak body on to the gurney, the baby had begun to crown.

"What's your name, honey?" The nurse was a heavy Black woman with a gold tooth in the front of her mouth.

"Jackie. Jackie Johnson."

"Date of birth?" The nurse asked.

"March 2, 1965." She lied again.

The nurse looked down at her face seeing her obvious youth filled face. Sensing Corrine's discomfort, the nurse instructed the orderlies to place her in the birthing room in the ER.

Corrine had decided to keep her identity and this baby a secret forever. No one would ever know that this had happened to her. Two hours and fourteen minutes later, Corrine gave birth to a baby boy. Five pounds even. Twenty inches long. Corrine barely got a glimpse of him when they placed him on her heaving chest. She had given birth to her first child in a strange hospital, with assistance of nurse and a doctor, in secret.

`The attending nurse came in periodically to check on her after the birth.

"How are you feeling?" She asked. Corrine didn't respond. She stared out the window wondering how she had gotten herself into this position.

"I'm fine." She said softly.

"Is there anyone that you'd like me to call Jackie?"

Jackie? Who's Ja…

Corrine had forgotten that she had given the nurse a fake name.

"No. There's no one to call." Corrine said.

"Well, in about an hour, a social worker is going to come down to chat with you. She'll just gather a bit of information." The nurse said. Corrine nodded.

"When will I be able to leave?"

"I don't know. That's a question for the doctor. You tore pretty bad, and he will want to make sure you don't have any complications. I'll ask, OK?"

Corrine nodded again. Corrine spent the day staring out the window. She wanted desperately to turn back time. She had gone to college to get an education, not to have a baby. She felt a wave of shame consume her. She thought about how her family and friends would view her, an unwed Black teenage mother. She was a statistic. Everything that she didn't want to be. One stupid decision had changed the entire trajectory of her life and she had to figure out how to reclaim herself.

The social worker knocked on the door of her room once, then entered.

"Jackie?" She inquired.

"Yes." Corrine said.

"Hi. I'm Cheryl and I wanted to come down and chat with you. Are you feeling up to it?" Corrine nodded.

"I won't be long." Cheryl reached into a bag and pulled out a yellow notepad and a blue Bic pen.

"Well, first, congratulations. You had a baby boy. Have you had time to bond with him?" Corrine shook her head, no.

"OK, well it's very important that you do that. Skin to skin contact stimulates his brain and his central nervous system. It will also aid him in his mental development. I'm going to encourage you to do that. OK?"

Corrine nodded again, this time, a small tear eked from her eye.

"Cheryl, I'm not keeping him. I can't."

Cheryl didn't seem surprised. "I figured that you were in distress, Jackie. In fact, the doctor requested that I come talk with you because he knew that you were in distress. Rarely does a crowning mother come into the hospital alone, and no one comes to visit after a baby is born. We see this more often than you can imagine, especially being so close to the university. I also suspect that your name isn't Jackie Johnson."

Corrine looked over to Cheryl with waterfall of tears coming from her eyes.

"Tell me what happened." Cheryl said.

Corrine proceeded to tell her the entire story. From the soirée to anemia, all the way up until she gave birth to her son. Cheryl sat quietly listening and taking notes.

"I can't take care of a baby Cheryl. I don't want to." Corrine felt horrible for saying that she didn't want to take care of her son. She was a child herself and she wasn't equipped emotionally to be a mother.

"There are options, Jackie."

"I know." Corrine said. Over the next few days, the two devised an adoption plan. Cheryl had introduced the idea of parenting to Corrine in several conversations, offering resources for financial and emotional aid. Corrine refused them all. She didn't want to be a mother, yet, and she couldn't bear the shame and judgment that she would surely receive. Adoption it was. Cheryl had the adoption unit attorney draft the documents that would relinquish Corrine's parental rights.

"We will need the father's signature too." Cheryl said. "How can we get in contact with him?"

Corrine felt a cold sweat overtake her body, "I don't know who the father is." She said hoping that that would stave off further inquiry. It did. Cheryl jotted another note and presented the documents to Corrine.

"By signing this document, you are agreeing to permanently and irreversibly terminate your parental rights to Baby Boy Johnson. Do you understand that?" Corrine sat up on the hospital bed with tears in her eyes, trembling, she said, "Yes." Cheryl continued to explain the document and instructed Corrine where to sign or initial. With the stroke of her pen, Corrine was no longer the mother of Baby Boy Johnson. She asked Cheryl what would happen now.

"Well, I am going to take this document to the attorney on site and she will give me another document allowing me to take the baby to the adoption agency. From there, they will find an appropriate family, and..."

Corrine held up her hand. The idea that that tiny life that she and Robert had created would be moved from her belly to a bassinet, to an agency, then to another home all in a few weeks of life, was too much for Corrine to wrap her head around.

"Can I see him?" Corrine said softly.

"Absolutely." Cheryl summoned the attending nurse to bring the baby to Corrine. She placed his tiny frame on her chest, and she wept. His breath smelled sweet, and she tried to take a mental picture of every part of his body. He laid on her chest for the better part of an hour before Cheryl spoke.

"Jackie? It's time." Corrine breathed in deeply and kissed the bottom of both of his feet. She said a silent prayer of protection and then handed him to Cheryl.

"Are you sure this is what you want?" Cheryl asked. *No, I'm not sure! I don't know what I want. God how am I going to live with this shame and sadness.* She thought.

"Yes. I'm sure," she said. In an instant, Cheryl wrapped the baby in a blue blanket and vanished from the room. Corrine sat in silence as she watched the sun set on the day, and her innocence. She would never be the same again.

21

Giving Thanks

Thanksgiving has always been my favorite holiday. Though it celebrates nothing, it's a time for families across America to get together, eat, play games, solve disputes, and, on occasion, drop bombshells. Thanksgiving is the perfect holiday for these things. Christmas is…well…Christmas and bombshells on Jesus' birthday seem harsh. Plus, Christmas is festive. Unlike Christmas, Thanksgiving is the throw away holiday that is attended, or not. It may include most of the family, or a small faction. It is usually subdued, and no one is required to bring a gift. It would be the perfect time to come clean to Corrine. I don't think that she suspected anything about me and Glenn, but I wanted her to hear and see us firsthand. I was a nervous wreck in the weeks leading up to it.

Years before, when Corrine was going through fertility treatments, I recall the same uneasiness. She was just about to start her second round of IVF and we had just gotten the news that James had to go to a officers training in California. He was going to be gone for two weeks. The window for IVF was small and he had already made his "contribution" the prior month. Corrine was scared and frustrated that she was going to have to do this treatment alone.

"I just can't believe that he's leaving, NOW!" She yelled.

Sam was at work and Corrine and I decided to ditch our respective jobs to have a girls' day. We sat in the quiet room at Serenity, a day spa in nearby Gretna. We frequented Serenity when we just needed a break from work, life, and for Corrine, the frustration of infertility. Sitting in our white fluffy robes and pink plastic spa sandals, sipping vanilla green tea, Corrine spoke softly.

"Momma, it's just too much. I am so tired of trying and I feel like I am being punished for something."

Corrine had confided in me before about their struggles to conceive, but I couldn't quite relate. Sam and I became pregnant soon after we got married and decided that we didn't want any more children after Corrine. When she was about 4, we revisited the idea but decided that one was enough. We were satisfied with our party of three. Corrine never expressed a desire to have siblings, but she was adamant about having a "house full of babies." Her dream of motherhood, she felt, was slipping through her fingers. The road was an exhausting and emotional rollercoaster every month. It began with great hope and expectation, only to be denied her desired outcome in the end.

Every month, for years, my daughter lived in a solitary hell, never expressing the excruciating emotional pain she was in, and the heavy burden of truth that she carried.

"Honey, I wish that I could make this pain all go away. I know that stressing over what hasn't happened won't make it happen any faster. We just have to pray and wait."

Corrine leaned her head back like it was made of lead.

"It's perfectly fine for you to be angry and sad. Don't you dare let anyone, including me, make you believe that your feelings aren't real. You have always been honest with me, and I intend to continue being honest with you," I said.

A single tear fell from Corrine's eye. She was ringing her hands and she opened her mouth, slightly, to speak. She remained silent.

"Did you want to say something, honey?" I asked.

She shook her head. I got up from my seat and went to her. I stood on her left and saw her eyes fixed on the ceiling.

"Momma, I need to tell you something."

Corrine was trembling. Her hands were clasped tightly together as she stared at the ceiling.

"OK. What do you need to say? I'm listening."

I placed my steady hands on her arm. Her body felt like a volcano about to erupt. I stood in silence waiting for Corrine to speak.

"It's OK, Corrine, I'm here. What do you want to tell me?"

I began to tremble too. I had never seen Corrine like this. What could she possibly need to say?

She took a deep breath and said, "Momma, I...I...I love you. That's all. I love you Mom."

Corrine was weeping. She didn't make a sound, but the flood of tears soaked the thick collar of her white robe. I reached down and hugged her tight. She was still trembling. My instincts told me that she wanted to say more, but I didn't press the issue. She was having a difficult time in her life and the last thing she needed was me, pressuring her to say more than she wanted.

"I love you too." I whispered in her ear. Almost instantly, Corrine composed herself and shook me off of her now steady body.

"I'm looking forward to this massage. Are you?"

"Yes," I said as I walked slowly back to my reclining seat. My mind was racing.

"Tomorrow is a big day. Fingers crossed that this IVF takes, Momma. I believe that we are going to have us a baby." She said with a smile.

"Yes, Corrine. Tomorrow is the beginning of the rest of your life."

We arrived at the fertility clinic 30 minutes early. Corrine knew the routine and she navigated the office like a pro. Forms were filled out, vitals were taken, money was paid, and then Corrine was led back in the office by a friendly Hispanic nurse with a beautiful head of long, dark, silky hair.

"Miss Corrine, is today the day, my love?" Corrine smiled and nodded.

"Yep. Today is the day!"

"I have been praying for you and James. You have been relaxing, yes?"

"Yes. My mom and I went to the spa yesterday and I have been taking walks, meditating, and taking my vitamins faithfully."

"Good, very good. Will mommy be joining us today?"

Corrine looked over at me, "Mom? Do you want to come?" Corrine looked hopeful that I would oblige.

"Sure. I don't know what I am supposed to do, but I'll be in there with you."

My heart began to race. I didn't know what to expect and the beige walls seemed to close in on me. I stood up from the green leather chair and began walking toward the open office door.

"Not yet, mommy." The nurse said. "Corrine has to get ready and the doctor too. I will come out when it's your turn to come in."

Corrine and the nurse walked through the door and disappeared as it slowly closed shut. I looked around the office searching for something to calm my nerves. The room was neutral. Everything matched. The walls matched the chairs, and the chairs match the brown, beige, and green, watercolor painting that hung on the walls. The coffee table was full of strategically placed magazines. They were displayed like playing cards at a poker game, fanned evenly, and organized. Rows of pamphlets lined the wall next to the glass reception desk. *IVF for Y.O.U.*, *IUI vs IVF*, *Infertility and You.* There was a model of the female anatomy on a tall wooden bookshelf, prominently displayed like a trophy. I had never had this experience and I was honored that Corrine invited me in.

The nurse popped through the door.

"OK mommy, we need you." I rose and was guided into a dressing room. "You need to put this on, and cover your hair too. Put the booties on your feet. Your purse is safe here. Let me know when you're ready."

She had placed a folded blue paper robe on a bench. I took off my sweater and placed it on the other end of the bench, then slid on the robe, arms first. The plastic strings to tie it taut across my waist were easily torn so I did my best to make sure they stayed intact. I slipped the blue paper booties over my Ferragamo flats and the hair covering onto my head.

"OK, I'm ready."

The nurse reemerged and said, "Blue is your color mommy."

I tried to laugh, but my nerves were too heightened. She led me into a room where my daughter laid, flat on her back, with her legs in stirrups. A small rolling silver tray was next to her shoulder and a drape separated her upper and lower body.

I stood by her side, "How you doing?" I asked nervously.

"Just another day of baby making." Corrine said sarcastically.

I grabbed her hand and squeezed it. Just then, with a single knock at the door, the tension was broken.

"Helloooo, Corrine! How are you? And who is this lovely lady?"

"Hi Dr. Diaz, this is my mother, Doris Ashworth." I nodded.

"It's very nice to meet you."

"You too. You have a wonderful daughter. We are missing someone, yes? Where is James?"

"Out of town. Mom is James today."

"Well," Dr. Diaz said, "she's a whole lot prettier than him!"

I laughed out loud, not because what he said was funny, but because I had to release the nervous energy that had reached a fever pitch.

"Well, we are glad that you are here Corrine, but we hope that we don't see you for another treatment for a very long time…at least a year."

Dr. Diaz began preparing himself and the instruments for the IVF.

"Now mommy, I need you to stay above the curtain. I'll handle what's below, OK?"

"Yes."

Dr. Diaz began calling out to the nurse terms that I didn't understand. He sat on a rolling bench and swirled around the room like a dancer. Opening drawers, pulling out instruments, swabs, drapes, and a speculum.

He slid next to me, grabbed the chart from the silver table and began reading, "Corrine...IVF...Embryo # 4578, 4789, 5623... Gravida 3...Parity 1...Temperature 98.7...BP 116/90. OK... everything looks good. Let's begin. You know the routine, Corrine."

Dr. Diaz washed his hands and put latex examination gloves on. He rolled his bench to the bottom end of the bed.

"Slide down just a bit Corrine." Corrine eased her way toward him.

"Perfect. OK...deep breath."

What felt like hours was only about 30 minutes. Dr. Diaz emerged from behind the drape as he was removing his gloves and disposing them in the red trash can labeled, *Biological Material*.

"All done. Corrine, you know the routine. I need you to stay put for a while. I'm also going to get you a prescription of progesterone." Dr. Diaz was at the sink washing his hands. "You'll need to take it after about 8 weeks. You'll be back here before then, but I want to make sure that you have it when you need it. Take it easy and limit your activity and stress. Got it?"

Corrine heard him, but I don't think she was listening to anything Dr. Diaz said. I could see the anticipation in her face.

"Yes, doctor," she said.

"OK, well then, I will see you in a couple days. It was lovely meeting you, Mrs. Ashworth." He patted me on my arm and looked in Corrine's eyes. "Stay hopeful."

"I will," Corrine said.

After dressing and saying our goodbye's, we walked from Dr. Diaz's office toward the car. "How do you feel?" I asked.

"Pregnant." Corrine said.

Oh, how I hoped she was. In that tummy could be my first grandchild. "Oh I hope so, Corrine. God knows I do."

22

Buns and Ovens

Thanksgiving that year came and went. We had celebrated as a family and had the usual fun, food, games, fights, and football. My sister and her husband had come down and some of James' family joined us as well. No one could really focus on anything other than Corrine. She was hell bent on hosting the holiday and wanted to cook everything. James and I had convinced her to stay off of her feet and she did, after she offered a strong objection.

"I'm not an invalid. Dr. Diaz said I could do a little."

"Cooking dinner for 20 is not a little anything," I objected.

We were successful in having her sit down, only after we compromised by allowing her to set the table. Boy, was she stubborn.

A month later, we were preparing for Christmas. Sam and I had secretly started buying baby clothes. Corrine had stopped doing that after the first failed round of IVF. It was just too painful for her. We also decided to get she and James the book, *What To Expect When Your Expecting*. It was supposed to be the ultimate guide to pregnancy, birth, and the first few months of a baby's life. To me, it was comedic. Writing a book that teaches you how to raise a child is like writing a book about how to sneeze. Ridiculous. But Corrine had heard that it was well-worth the $26.95 that the paid for it. We wrapped the gifts but stashed them away in the hall closet. We had no intention of giving them to Corrine and James unless and until they were pregnant. We prayed they were.

Our family tradition was to celebrate Christmas Eve with just me, Sam, Corrine, and James. Each of us was allowed to open one present. It was a tradition that started when I was a child. My parents would allow each one of the children to open a gift. Usually, it was the pajamas that my mother had made for us to sleep in that night. Sam and I had carried the tradition for Corrine, and although our little family didn't have any children in it, we continued it.

Christmas music bellowed in the house, and Corrine and James handed us our gifts. "You two have to open your gifts at the same time," they demanded. The house was warm and comfy. Sam had decorated the outside with holly and evergreen wreaths. The fireplace provided the perfect lighting and the sound of the crackling wood soothed me. Sam and I sat with a small square package on our laps.

"OK," Corrine said.

"On the count of three, 1-2-3." Sam and I tore into the package and a white box peeked from beneath the shiny red wrapping paper. We looked at each other, and on cue, we opened the boxes.

"Bread? You got us a piece of bread?"

Sam pulled the hard roll out of the box, "And they didn't give us any butter!" We looked at Corrine and James for clarity. They both were smiling like Cheshire cats.

"Mom…it's not a roll." I stared and my gift again.

"A biscuit?" Corrine and James threw their heads back in frustration.

"Mom, what's another word for bread and biscuit?"

I sat thinking when Sam chimed in, "Bun?"

Corrine and James said, "YES!" in unison.

Sam and I stared at them, even more confused.

"You got me a bun? Why?" Sam said.

"Well, mine is cold, I'm gonna put it in the…wait!"

"Bun in the oven? There's a bun in the oven?" I screamed, "I'm going to be a grandmother!!!"

We were ecstatic. I jumped up and hugged Corrine. Tears were running down her face. We wept and laughed together.

"Oh wait…wait…Sam, go get the…the…presents! Oh, hurry Sam."

Sam went to the closet and pulled out the boxes.

"We've been shopping a little." James and Corrine laughed.

"What in the hell!" Corrine and James opened each gift and "ooooeeedddd and awweeeddd."

We spent the rest of the evening listening to Corrine and James plan the life of their forming child. Sam fell asleep with a onesie resting on his belly, and I perused *What To Expect When You're Expecting*. I watched as each one of my family members fell asleep. The idea that next Christmas, we would have a little baby in the family, filled me with joy. I thumbed through the book. My reading focused on a section entitled, *Terms To Remember*.

"Gravida and para (parity) are medical terms related to pregnancy and birth. Gravida describes the total number of confirmed pregnancies. Para or parity is defined as the number of births that a woman has had after 20 weeks of gestation."

I sat up in my chair. *Wait…what?* I knew that Corrine had

experienced 2 miscarriages, but they were well before 20 weeks. Parity. Dr. Diaz said parity, 1. *Corrine had a pregnancy that lasted 20 weeks?* I instantly hearkened back to the day at the spa. Maybe that's what she was trying to tell me. I looked over at her as she slept in the arms of James on the couch. *Good lord, I need to talk to her...or maybe I don't. My heart broke for her. My baby had a baby? But where was this child?*

23

Lights, Flashing, Lights

Coming to terms with my own truth was a long process. I hadn't seen Glenn in months. We talked on the phone periodically, but I had work to do on myself and as much as I missed him, I didn't want to lose me in the petals of our budding love. Now that I was in a better place, we had started seeing each other again. At first, we eased into it, but that wasn't our nature. I wanted him more and I was now free to give myself to him, completely and out loud. We had no idea that what we had tried to keep hidden, was known and out in the open for all of Hilbrand to see and talk about. I feared that Corrine would find out about me and Glenn before I had the chance to tell her myself. I knew how damaging secrets could be in a family, and I didn't want to be the cause of any pain for my already wounded daughter.

But then, my thought would turn to Glenn. My Glenn. Sometimes the very thought of him caused lightning bolts to flash between my eyes, into my heart, and landing squarely between my legs. Our love had now grown to a point where sex was no longer the goal, but rather intimacy. We had grown into each other. Our bodies had become familiar, and they spoke their own language. I could tell by the look in his eyes what he was thinking. He, when we were together, could read the sway of my hips to know exactly when I would climax. That's the benefit of getting old. You pay closer attention to details. You focus on the journey rather than the destination. I could read small shifts in his weight or thrusts of his hips like a book. I studied him and he, me. Most days, we didn't have to have intercourse. Many a night we spent time just exploring the body of the other. He had even showered me once.

I stood naked as the water poured over my skin. Glenn sat on the bench behind me and scrubbed my skin end to end. The suds offered a slick road for the exfoliating body gloves that he wore. His gentle touch awakened my pores and caused me to relax into his grasp. He rinsed me off and led my wet nude body to my bed. He laid me down and spent an hour rubbing me with my signature coconut oil. It was the most intimate thing I had ever experienced. His hands were curious, and he used them to become intimately acquainted with me. All of me. I was no longer ashamed or afraid to have the lights on. In fact, I loved seeing us in the light. By no means were we perfect, but our bodies had seen decades of history and every line, bump, lump, and shape held a story. He was beautiful to me. His dark skin against my brown was the perfect swirl. Yes, Glenn knew me inside and out, and he could please me even with my clothes on.

Hearing his knock at the door caused a frenzy inside. I looked forward to him. Seeing him. Smelling him. And having him hold me. That night that he waited outside of my door, our first night, was the beginning of this beautiful love affair, one that I never thought possible, especially now. We were inseparable by now, so it was no surprise that right before Thanksgiving, Glenn made a proposition one night after we had made love.

"I have an idea." He always came up with these brilliant ideas after one of our love making sessions. I propped myself up and rested my head on his chest. He spoke sweetly, while stroking my hair. I felt the warmth of his skin against my cheek and our legs were intertwined like spaghetti.

"What's your brilliant idea, Glenn?"

He took a deep breath, "What if I come to Thanksgiving with you? You know, with the family?"

A cold bead of sweat formed on my forehead. I could feel that he was holding his breath, waiting for my answer.

I hesitated, " I don't think that's a good idea."

He exhaled, "Why not? We are a couple, right? And couples spend holidays together. Unless of course. We're not."

"No sweetheart, we absolutely are...but..." I hesitated more because I didn't have the heart to tell him that I hadn't spoken about him to anyone except Nia. Corrine had no idea that I had been seeing Glenn. I couldn't tell her. I just didn't think Corinne was ready to hear that there was another man in my life.

I sat up, "Glenn, it's only been a year and a half since her father died. You have to understand what it feels like for her." As the words escaped from my mouth, I didn't believe them. This wasn't about Corrine. The fear was in me. I was content living in our little bubble, but Glenn wanted our relationship public. How would that look? Why did I care? What would everyone say?

"You treat her like some desperate, wounded teenager. She's a grown ass woman, Doris. I know that she misses her dad and you miss Sam too, but I'm here." Glenn had never raised his voice, but his volume was higher than I had ever experienced it.

192

"It's just not a good idea, honey. Maybe Christmas."

Glenn slowly released me from his grasp and sat on the edge of the bed. He shook his head in frustration. The perfect black skin on his back glistened in the moonlight. I eased over to caress him around his waist, my head at his left hip. I gently kissed his oblique muscle.

"Don't be angry. It's just so soon."

"Too soon? Really Doris? I've been in your bed now every day. For months. What more do you want from me to have me in your whole life? And on top of that, I love you." He turned his head to look at me. "Doris, I'm in love with you. Did you hear me? I'm in love with you."

I released my grip from around his waist and lay flat on my back. He turned more to me as one tear dropped from my eye and rolled like a river to my temple. I was in love with him too.

"I'm in love with you too, but I'm just not sure I should be."

He threw his hand up in frustration and stood up to dress. As he slipped on his pants, he turned to me, shirtless.

"You're going to have to make a decision about what you want. I know this situation is hard with your daughter, but the truth is that you have lived your life for her and everyone else for too long. If you want me, I'm right here."

I didn't respond. I didn't know how to.

That afternoon, after Glenn left, irritated. With the holiday issue unresolved, I summoned Nia to the house. She arrived at 1:00 PM as agreed. I greeted her at the door before she could put her key in the lock. My expression spoke volumes.

"Gram, what's going on? You never call me to come over. What is going on?" She looked concern. We sat knee to knee. She on her grandfather's chair, me on the ottoman.

"Nia, Glenn said the words."

"What words Gram?"

"I'm in love with you."

"Whatttttttttttt?" Nia asked while she leaned back in the chair and raised her hands to the sky. "Oh shiitttt Gram! I thought y'all was just fuckin'! I didn't know it was like THAT! Like love, love. I mean the whole ice on the kitchen island thang didn't look like love!"

I cut her a look. "Watch your mouth little girl. I'm still your grandmother! And I don't ever want to hear the word ice come out of your mouth again!" I slapped her on her knee.

"My bad Gram." She motioned like she was washing her mouth out. "So what did you say back?"

"I said what I said." She looked at me quizzically. "I said that I loved him too."

Nia squealed like a greased piglet. "Alright now Gram! I see you getting yo' groove back and whatnot! Go 'head nah!" She stopped and looked at my stoic face. She calmed. "Do you love him?"

" Yes, I do. I just don't know if I'm allowed to yet. Your grandfather's only been dead for a year and a half. It seems like it's just too soon for me to be in love with someone else."

I felt uneasy and nervous. Nia grabbed both of my hands in hers and squeezed them.

"Gram, I'm about to tell you something that may hurt your feelings. But I want you to understand the intention behind what I'm saying. OK?"

Nia looked serious. She had always been jovial when we talked about Glenn, but this was a different countenance. I braced myself.

"What do you have to say?"

She steadied herself.

"Pop-Pop died 5 years ago. The day that he was diagnosed, Pop-Pop died."

I lowered my head and began to weep.

"And Gram, I never saw you as happy as you are now, even before his Cancer. Gram, I'm not sure you've ever been in love."

By now I was sobbing.

"I think you and Pop-Pop loved each other, but I'm not sure you were ever in love with him."

My head was resting in Nia's lap. I had never considered that my life, the one that was mapped out for me by society, family, and my faith, was unfulfilling. I was a puppet. Sam was a good husband and father, and I was with him because in my day, that's what women did. I always felt the emptiness, but I had never spoken it out loud. Nia saw me sobbing in my truth and for the first time, I felt the depth and breadth of it. I laid in her lap and felt like I was purging the dead weight of expectation and obligation that I held for 50 years. She was right. I'd never been in love with Sam. I loved him, had children with him, and stayed committed to him, but he had never seen me for me. It was a role, I was a performer for 50 years, 4 months, and 27 days. How was I going to explain to Corrine that my life with her father had been a lie? How could she ever forgive me for not being my whole self? What would she say when I told her that I was in love with another man? My secret had to be revealed and there was no time to waste.

Nia and I talked all night. We ordered food and had it delivered. She convinced me to call Glenn and invite him to Thanksgiving.

"If you're gonna reclaim your life Gram, do it boldly. Mom will be fine...or not!"

I nodded in agreement. I needed to live my life for me, not for my child, my granddaughter, Sam, or Glenn. It was my turn to do what I wanted to do, with whom I wanted to do it. I reached for the phone and called Glenn. His voice on the speakerphone filled the room.

"Hello?"

"Baked turkey or fried?"

Nia was staring right in my face as I proposed dinner to Glenn.

"What?"

"For Thanksgiving...with my family...what do you want to eat? Baked or fried turkey?"

He stayed silent for a moment then let out a chuckle and cleared his throat, "Neither. The only thing I want to eat, is you."

I blushed and tried to quickly find the button to take him off the speakerphone. Nia's eyes widened in shock, and she slid down the chair like melting ice cream. I closed my eyes, embarrassed and blissful.

"I'll call you later, Glenn."

24

Out of the Darkness, Into the Marvelous Light

Nia and I started shopping for Thanksgiving on Wednesday. Every year we vow never to go to the store the day before and every year we end up standing in hour long checkout lines with throngs of other people who wait to shop for Thanksgiving dinner.

"Nia, this is going to be horrible…or wonderful…right?" I hadn't been that nervous in years. In fact, I don't think I have ever been that nervous. I was a grown woman and I was introducing my boyfriend to my family. *Boyfriend. When you're 73, are you allowed to have a boyfriend?*

"Look Gram," Nia said as she pushed the shopping cart through the produce aisle, "Corrine is gonna have something to say, you already know this. You just have to speak your truth." I nodded as I selected a bag of yellow onions and put them in the basket.

"And, there's no turning back now. Your booyyyyyfffrriennddd is coming over whether she likes it or not." Nia giggled with glee. "Child this is going to be a show! Corrine is gonna have a goat!"

We arrived back at my house, and we unloaded the groceries. The phone rang. I reached over the bags to grab it.

"Hello?"

"Hey mom!" It was Corrine.

"I'm making the cutest turkey place cards for the table and wanted to make sure that was OK. I don't want to mess up your décor."

I put my hand over the mouthpiece. I stared wide-eyed at Nia. She mouthed

"What?"

"She's making place cards," I whispered.

"So?" Nia said matter-of-factly. I stared at her more intently. "Ooohhhhh."

My eyes widened and I grunted.

"OK, tell her that you have a guest coming." Nia smiled slyly. I took a deep breath and pulled my hand away from the phone.

"Yes, dear. It's fine. But I have asked a friend to join us for dinner so can you make another one?" Nia was doubled over laughing silently. I scolded her with my eyes.

"Oh, how nice mom. It's good that you are making friends."

"Yes, well." Corrine had no idea how *good* it was.

"So what's your friends name?"

I steadied myself. "Glenn…like Close."

"Glenn?" Corrine asked.

"Yes. Glenn…2 Ns…like Close." I waited for her to ask for more details about Glenn. She didn't.

"OK. I'll make one for Miss Glenn. James and I will see you Thursday. Love you."

Miss Glenn. Yes. That's right, Corrine. Miss Glenn. My heart was pounding. *Tell her the truth now, Doris.* I thought to myself. Nope. Not yet. When he walks through the door, she'll know that

Glenn is a WHOLE mister. I'll tell her then.

"Love you too." I pushed the end button on the phone and Nia burst into hysterics.

"Glenn…like Close? Really Gram?"

"Listen, your mother will find out on Thursday. I just need to keep her occupied until then. If she thinks Glenn is a woman, then that's on her. I didn't lie, I just didn't tell the whole truth."

Nia doubled over in laughter.

Corrine was excited to add a pop of elegance to the Thanksgiving table. She had the place cards professionally made and now, needed to have a rush order done to accommodate my new friend, Glenn. Though it was short notice, she ran past Tyler's Trophy shop to order one more acrylic card bearing the name *Glenn*. She had made it to the shop at about 3:00 PM and spoke directly to Mr. Tyler. My Tyler was an old African American man with rounded shoulders and a piecey gray beard.

"Mr. Tyler I need another card by tonight. My mother invited a new friend over to the house for Thanksgiving."

"How nice. It's good that she is making friends. How long has it been since…?"

"About 2 years, but it sometimes feels like just yesterday." Corrine held back her tears and continued her request of Mr. Tyler.

"So, I need the name *Glenn* on a card just like the others. Can I get it by close of business today?"

"Glenn, you say? THAT's the friend?"

Corrine cocked her head in confusion. "Yes, my mother said that she was bringing her girlfriend, Glenn to dinner on Thursday."

Mr. Tyler laughed nervously.

"Unless your mom has an affinity for people named Glenn, then the Glenn she's talking about is a man."

A man?

"A man? That's impossible. Why would my mother be friends with a man? My parents were married for 50 years, and all of their friends were couples. I have never heard of a Glenn."

Mr. Tyler continued.

"Well all I know is a few months ago, I saw your mother walking hand-in-hand from the Darden Grill with Glenn Spears. She got in her car, and I think he kissed her. Don't quote me, but I've heard that they have been seeing each other for a while."

Corrine grew hot with anger.

"You must be mistaken."

"No, I don't think I am." Mr. Tyler was gathering the acrylic from a small bin. He selected a piece that was the perfect size for him to cutout the turkey shape. His back was turned to Corrine as he polished and etched the small clear card.

"I think it's good for her. Old folks think they have to shrivel up into nothingness when they lose a spouse or a child. Your mom still has a life to still lead. I say **Hell Yes** for finding another companion."

Corrine was seething so much that she couldn't speak. As Mr. Tyler finished the carving, he held it to the light to ensure that there weren't scratches or blemishes.

"There. That was easy." He turned back to Corrine. "That'll be $8.50." Corrine pulled a $10.00 bill out of her purse.

"Keep the change."

Before Mr. Tyler could say a proper goodbye, Corrine was at the door pulsating with anger and embarrassment. She got in her car and called me.

"Hello?"

"Mother, we need to talk."

The next morning, Corrine arrived at my house with James. Nia had spent the night, as always, sleeping on the floor. She and I brined the turkey, peeled sweet potatoes, cleaned greens, and cut up the members of the "holy trinity" for the dressing. I opened the door. I could immediately sense that something was wrong. Corrine stood erect, clutching her purse and a gift bag filled with acrylic place cards.

"Happy Thanksgiving!" I yelled. Corrine pushed past me, saying nothing. James reached down and kissed me.

"Brace yourself, mom."

I closed the door behind James and walked toward Corrine.

"Happy Thanksgiving honey."

She looked at me, stone-faced, "Who is Glenn mom?"

My heart dropped and a knot formed in my throat.

"A friend. Just a friend."

"A friend? Well do you kiss all of your *friends.*"

Nia stood up and whispered, "Awwww shit."

"I don't know what you're talking about Corrine."

She slammed her purse down on the easy chair.

"Oh you don't know what I'm talking about? Well, the word around town is that my mother is gallivanting around with some strange man."

My body felt weak.

"My God, mother, daddy isn't even cold yet and you are shaming this family by being seen with this Glenn person. Who is he mom? Where did you meet?"

I stumbled over my words.

"Calm down Corrine."

"YOU CALM DOWN!" She yelled. "My daddy died, and you're walking around here without a care in the world. You have disgraced our family and dishonored daddy's memory too. For goodness sake, mother, you are a 73 year-old widow, mother, and grandmother. Sit yo' ass down and stop acting like a horny teen!" Corrine's voice cracked. I tried to console her, but she wasn't interested in anything I had to say. I looked at Nia and she motioned to me to say something.

"Corrine? OK. OK. I know this is a lot to take in." I didn't have the words to calm her down. "I know this is a shock, but honey, it's different and special. I have been seeing a man. Glenn is…"

I couldn't get the rest of my words out. As I was trying to muster up the right thing to say, the doorbell rang. I felt the color drain from my face. Nia motioned for me to get the door. I wiped my hands on my apron and turned the knob. I remember feeling the same butterflies in my stomach that first night Glenn appeared at my door. This time, however, the flutter of butterflies was replaced with the panic of crows. I opened the door and there he stood wearing a black sweater and black slacks. His bright white smile hypnotized me for just a second. With his arms outstretched, he leaned in to give me a hug. I pushed him away. His face grew confused.

"Corrine and James are here. She knows." I whispered.

Glenn fanned his hands gesturing me to let him in. As he crossed the threshold, Corrine turned to look at him.

"Um…hello everyone. Nia?"

"Heyyyyyy Mr. Glenn." Nia said "We were just talking about

you."

Corrine and I both cut her a look. She giggled to herself.

"And you must be James." Glenn reached out to shake James' hand and he reciprocated. Corrine gave James a look of disdain.

"Awww…and you must be Corrine. I have heard so much about you," Glenn said.

"Funny, I don't know anything about you. Hell, I didn't even know you existed until yesterday." Corrine said flatly.

My eyes darted toward her then back to Glenn. "We…we were just talking about how you and I met and how we are friends." I clenched my teeth together signaling to Glenn to keep the details of our relationship under wraps.

"Ye…yes…me and your mom are good friends." Glenn replied.

James had turned on the TV to watch football. His disinterest in the subject made Corrine even more angry.

"Corrine, may I see you in the bedroom please." With her coat still on, Corrine walked past the kitchen where Nia was trying to shrink into nothing, so she didn't catch a ricochet of Corrine's wrath.

"Sure momma. Let's talk."

I followed behind her.

We stood in the bedroom where me and Glenn had laid together the day before, the remnants of our encounter on the pile of sheets in the laundry basket behind Corrine. I cleared my throat.

"Listen, I'm sorry I didn't tell you about Glenn. There was just never a good time. Everything happened so fast and…"

"Save it mom. I'm just disgusted. Your husband died less than 2 years ago, you're hiding this man and this relationship from me, and you are a totally different person. I have never kept ANYTHING from you! Ever. I just can't believe how irresponsible you're being. I mean, who is this guy and what does he want?"

She was livid. Her rage turned to sadness, her sadness to despair.

"He's a stranger, momma! You haven't even grieved for daddy yet, and now you are cavorting with some guy around town?"

I had raised my child, been a faithful wife, and supported everyone in my life. It's my turn. My blood was boiling. Why couldn't she see how happy I was?

"You are the last person that needs to speak about keeping secrets. Corrine. You have a few of your own." Corrine stopped in her tracks and looked at me with fear in her eyes.

"I am a grown woman." I breathed deeply. "Listen, your dad died long before his diagnosis. He stopped being my husband that day. I became his nurse. Now, don't get me wrong, I loved your father. He was an extraordinary man, but Corrine, I am in love with Glenn. I know that it seems odd, but I haven't been free to be me my whole life. I have lived longer than I will, and I want to live with joy and…well…sex too! There I said it! S.E.X."

"Oh my God, mother! You're having sex with this man?" Corrine flopped back on my bed.

"Yes."

Realizing that she was laying on my bed and deducing that some of our escapades had taken place where she lay, she popped up.

"In this house? In this bed? Who are you? I just can't... These lies and secrets. It's just too much." Corrine was pacing the floor, waving her hands and brushing her shoulders like she was wiping the stench of our encounters off of her clothes.

We were yelling back and forth. James came in the room to gain control of a very out-of-control situation. My anger had detonated and exploded all over our house.

"Secrets and lies? Really Corrine? You wanna talk about secrets and lies? OK. Where's the baby?"

James, with his hands outstretched to hush the rage, turned to Corrine. Her face turned white, and she dropped to her knees.

"Corrine!" I yelled. I knelt down beside her.

She was sobbing uncontrollably. I grabbed my daughter in my arms and rocked her. Nia rushed in with Glenn.

Nia yelled, "What the hell is going on in here?" She joined us on the floor.

Corrine sobbed for several minutes, and we waited. *Lord, what have I done? I let my rage get the best of me and now my daughter is in a puddle of tears, broken.*

"Oh momma, I tried so many times to tell you." Her voice was soft and cracking. "It was college. I didn't know what to do. I don't know where he is."

I began to sob.

"What are you talking about mom?" Nia asked.

Corrine scooted over to Nia. "You have a brother."

That night, Corrine told Nia everything. James, I learned later in the evening, knew about the baby that Corrine had so many years ago. Nia sat still and quiet. "I have a brother?" James sat in silence and wore the same Stepford smile that he had on their wedding day. Once again, he was realizing that he was still an accessory in Corrine's "perfect" life.

Corrine crawled to her daughter. "Nia, your whole life.

Everything I did. Everything I didn't do was to try to redeem myself for the mistake that I made. I never wanted you to hate me for placing your brother, but I was so ashamed of myself that I created a lie and I lived in it. You picked up the tab for my shame."

Nia looked down at her mother and saw her, for the first time, as a woman. Not a mother, but as a woman. She was in shock. "All my life I tried to live up to a standard that you set for me that you didn't hold yourself to." She continued. "I played the role as long as I could and when I decided to be my authentic self, you walked away from me." Nia stood, seemingly towering over her mother. "Not only have you put me in a box my whole life, you put Gram in one too. Your whole life has been a lie. From the Highlands to this baby. Everything."

Corrine sat weeping in my chest, while James and Glenn stood behind us rubbing our backs. Three generations of women in the same family living with secrets and lies. Avoiding their own truth for the sake of appearances. We had all sought the shadows for fear of the sun exposing our true selves to the world.

"Mom, I can't say that I forgive you. What I can say is, I love you." Nia reached out to hold her mother's hand.

Glenn was standing next to me as I was still sitting on the floor. He reached for my hand and pulled me up. He embraced me tightly and I wept. I could feel the eyes of my family on us, and I feared their faces when I turned around. When I turned, they were gone. They had all left the room. It was just Glenn and I, alone. He kissed my forehead, pulled away from me, then held my face in his hands and kissed me passionately on my lips. Our love was no longer in the shadows. It was out in the open, basking in the glow of the sun.

25

Blinded by the Light

Over the next several weeks, Glenn and I kept our romance alive and in public. Corrine had warmed up to the idea, but by no means was she a full fan of our love affair. She asked that I not discuss the details of our relationship, and I vowed not to. I understood that it was just too painful for her to hear about another man in my life and my bed.

She and Nia had another cross to bear. The idea of having an older brother somewhere in the world consumed Nia's every thought. She would confide in me about her disdain and anger toward her mother.

"She made my life hell. She tried to right her wrongs on my back." Nia became angry and even more resentful of Corrine. I watched my granddaughter shrink into bitterness and pain. The exercise class was coming to an end and the friendships that I had gained from my time there were too. We all knew that we would go our separate ways once Nia called "Time" on our last class. It was bittersweet. I lost 30 pounds and gained a tremendous amount of strength and according to Glenn, my stamina was off the charts!

One Saturday morning, I went for a long walk by myself. I

reflected on my life. How this journey began and how now, I was living as a new, independent, happy woman. My role had been defined. I am a woman. I got to my favorite part of the park. The crisp air pierced my ears and the caramel sun gleamed off the pond that was surrounded by tall trees with a Crayola box of colored leaves. I sat on the wood slat bench to take in the beauty of the day. A family of ducks swam in a perfect row and the smell of Spring was wafting through my nose. I breathed in deeply and prayed. *Dear God, Thank you.* I had never been so happy in all my life. Sitting in the silent stillness of the morning, I was startled when my phone rang and vibrated in my pocket. I fumbled to answer it.

"Hello?"

"Gram, I did it! I finished my thesis. I'm done!" Nia was silly with joy. I could hear the sweet relief in her voice.

"Yes sweetheart! I am so proud of you!"

"Yeah Gram, my professor told me that my thesis was one of the most well-researched that he has ever seen. He thinks that I should continue my work and keep the class going. In fact, he said that I should think about a doctorate in Gerontology."

"Wow Nia! That's amazing. We MUST celebrate!"

"We need to Gram…soon."

"Well, sweetheart, I love you."

"I love you too Gram." She hung up the phone and I couldn't help but smile. Just as I was putting it back in my pocket, the phone rang again.

"Hello?"

"Gram, I have to find him." She sounded somber.

I knew who Nia was talking about.

"Who sweetheart?"

"My brother. I have to find him."

"That's a tough one Nia. If you want to, you're going to have to talk to your mom about...all of it. Are you ready to do that?"

"Gram, my whole life I was made to believe that I wasn't what they wanted me to be. I wasn't smart enough, or pretty enough. I was too wild. I was too different. Stand up straight. Cross your legs. Everything I did was scrutinized. I could never make her happy or proud. Now I know why. She was in pain from her placing her son up for adoption and I was a constant reminder of her secret. I need to find him to close the circle and hopefully help her heal, and me too." Nia was sincere. The morning sun was peering out from behind the trees and the sun was in my face.

"Sweetheart, I will be with you every step of the way. We have to talk to your mom and see what she wants to do."

"No!" Nia shouted. "I need to find him for me. My mom held this in for almost 30 years, and it's time to get the truth. I'm not asking her anything. I'm telling her that I am going to find my brother."

That night, as I lay next to Glenn, I told him about the conversation that I had with Nia.

"Doris, she deserves to know. I can't say that I disagree with her." He stroked my shoulder and gently kissed my hand.

"This isn't going to be easy."

"Nothing ever is Doris. But I can tell you this," Glenn said, as he scooted his naked body closer to mine, "I will be with you every step of the way."

My body grew warmer.

" I love you, Doris Ashworth."

I turned toward him, our bodies close together and our eyes locked.

"I love you too, Glenn Spears."

9 780578 336886